MW00526297

Mr. Nightmare: II - The Nightmare Realm
By Joe Scipione

Wicked House Publishing

Cover design by Christian Bentulan
Interior Formatting by Joshua Marsella

For Mandy

CHAPTER 1

It was about time to revive the original Nightmare Club.

About two weeks after I graduated college the thought popped into my head. It was early June and I was back living at home with Mom and Dad when I had the idea. I'd kept in touch with Merrie and Marcus all through college, wrote them letters a couple times a year, talked to them—especially Merrie—on the phone and met up with them at holidays when I was home on break. Merrie hadn't gone away to college after high school. Instead, she got a job at a nursing home and was going to school part-time to be a nurse and was making really good money. She still lived with her parents and since I was at home too, we'd become neighbors again, living in the good old Prairie View neighborhood.

Marcus had graduated college a year before me and was living in an apartment on the other side of town, working at an insurance company. The point was, we were all in town and summer was on the horizon, just like when we first formed the Nightmare Club. Things were different now, but I wouldn't mind taking a walk out to the Dwelling with my oldest and closest friends.

"Some things don't change," Mom said as I sat at the

kitchen table lost in thought. She was where she almost always was when I was home: in the kitchen cooking. It was noon on a Tuesday and Dad was at work, meaning it was only Mom and I at the house for the day. It didn't matter than it was noon, it was my first meal of the day, so Mom was going to make me breakfast. I think she enjoyed having me home again, I'm sure part of her knew it was going to be a short-term thing until I got a job and a place of my own, but living at home had its perks.

"What do you mean?" I said, because I hadn't really been paying attention to what she was saying. I was thinking about the past and about my friends while Mom was talking.

"Finding a job after college," she said. She put a plate with a scrambled egg and two pieces of bacon in front of me and then sat at the other side of the table—in Chuck's chair—with a plate of her own. "I went to college for business. Couldn't find a job right away. Lived with my parents doing various jobs and temp stuff at various offices until I met your dad. Kept doing that until I got married and then got pregnant. The job search stopped there and I never really looked again. Now, here you are, looking for a job."

"Something will come up. There are always teaching jobs that open up through the year and I have my name in to substitute at all the local schools. I'm sure someone will leave in an English department in the fall and then I can just slide right in." I scooped a forkful of eggs into my mouth and took a sip of coffee.

"I hope so, Anna," Mom said. "Though I do like having you here. I'd never make eggs and bacon just for me." She smiled and we ate in silence for a bit.

"I think I'm going to try to meet up with Merrie and Marcus this week. I talk to them a lot but we haven't hung out, just the three of us, in a long time."

"That would be great!" Mom said. "I see Marcus sometimes in town. I think he must live up there now. And Merrie is doing very good from what people say. She's at the retirement home over off Washington Street."

"Yeah. It will be good to hang out with them." I had the last bite of breakfast.

"Leave your plate, I'll clean it up."

"Okay, I'm off to grab the Tribune, see if there are any new jobs today. Need anything from the store?"

"No, hun. I'm all set. See you later."

I got up from the table, grabbed the keys to my car out of my room and left.

The good thing about working as a substitute teacher the last three years of college, it meant I'd saved up enough money to buy a car. The bad thing about it was the pay was so low, I couldn't afford a very nice car. The 1985 Ford Escort I bought was used and had been run into the ground. The muffler barely worked, so anyone within a two-mile radius could hear me coming, and anyone in a five-mile radius knew when I turned the damned thing on. It got me from point A to point B so I couldn't complain. Every time I started it though, I thought of the day I'd have enough money to buy a car that didn't sound like a monster truck when I drove it—or better yet, a brand-new car.

I turned on the Dying Buffalo—the nickname my college friends had given to the brown monstrosity—and eased it down the driveway.

We lived about a ten-minute drive to the center of town and while it wasn't a small town, all the convenience stores were either in the center or on the north side. I turned on the radio and got lost in thought as I made the drive. Chuck and John weren't constantly in my thoughts when I was at school, but being home again made it hard to think about other things. I drove on the streets we used to walk as kids. I always slowed down when I passed the Field. Usually there was a group of kids hanging out at the basketball court or by the dugouts. When I saw them, I couldn't help but think about Chuck and

John. Chuck was gone. I'd watched them put him in the ground thanks to Mr. Nightmare. But John, John wasn't gone—not really anyway. I knew he was still out there somewhere. Looking for dreams—for nightmares. Sometimes everything that happened at the Dwelling and with Mr. Nightmare felt like a dream. I could almost convince myself that it *was* a dream. Then I'd think about Chuck and John and I'd know that it wasn't. It wasn't a *nightmare.* Everything that had happened to the Nightmare Club was real. Maybe someday John would come back one last time. Maybe he'd collect enough nightmares to appear here in this world again. I always held out hope of that.

It's possible I called Merrie and Marcus later on that night because I'd been thinking so much about John and Chuck. I'd asked them to meet because I missed them, but maybe it *was* time for another meeting of the Nightmare Club.

CHAPTER 2

W e met later that night at a pizza place not far from our neighborhood. Guild Street Pizza was a small bar/pizza place that was a fixture for us growing up. End-of-the-year team parties were always held there after basketball or softball season. It was close enough that the adults who lived in Prairie View could walk home if they had too much to drink, but for me it was the place Dad and I got pizza a few days after Chuck died. I'd never forget the drive home with the hot pizza box on my lap, trying to make my mind think of anything other than Chuck. I'd been back to Guild Street Pizza after that time of course, but it was always that trip I thought of.

I was supposed to meet Merrie and Marcus there at seven but I got there early because I was anxious to see them and needed to get out of the house. When I walked in the front door and looked for a table to sit at in the bar area, I was met with Merrie's smiling face waving with her hand high over her head. I smiled, happy to see her and weaved through the other tables to get to her.

"Hey there," she said, her smile grew even wider. She stood up when I got there and we hugged. It was good to see her.

"I thought I was going to be the first one here," I said after we greeted each other and sat down.

"I had to come right from work. If I go home after I just get tired and don't want to get back up. Good thing I had a change of clothes. Marcus should be on his way," she said. Marcus and Merrie had been on again-off again during high school, but once Marcus left for college and Merrie stayed behind, it didn't work out. They stayed close though, even after they broke up the last time, and I don't think things got awkward between them. At least, neither of them mentioned it to me.

Merrie and I talked for a while, catching up, me telling her about college and the so-far-unsuccessful job search and her telling me about the retirement home drama—which had nothing to do with the residents and everything to do with the staff. The conversation was easy—as it was every time we got together. Like we never missed a beat. We got so lost in our own conversation that we didn't even notice Marcus when he came up to our table.

"Well, if this doesn't remind me of old times, I'm not sure what does," Marcus said, putting his hands on both our shoulders before he spoke. We stood up and hugged him. He even gave Merrie and quick peck on the cheek. She didn't know it, but I caught the small smirk on her face as it happened. He sat down in the booth on Merrie's side. Again, there was another fast smile from her. We ordered drinks—beers for Marcus and I and Diet Coke for Merrie because she was twenty for another few months—and pizza, then we sat and talked for most of the night. As with Merrie and I, Marcus fell back into his old role within the group. We talked about our lives and told stories about the past, growing up and the things we did together, but none of us mentioned the Nightmare Club or Mr. Nightmare the entire time. There was too much laughing and smiling; bringing up that *other* part of our past would have put an end to the joviality. I was fine letting us have a good time for most of the night, but I wasn't going to let anyone leave without talking about that ugly part of our shared past.

We'd had a good amount to drink in the few hours we'd been there. The pizza we'd ordered was gone and I'd had four beers—though Merrie had stolen sips from them so it was probably more like two and a half, and Marcus drank about the same as me. We were feeling good and still having a good time. When there was a lull in the conversation, I took the opportunity to bring up the other reason I wanted to see them.

"So, listen guys," I said. I wanted to make my tone easygoing, but they knew me too well and the mood changed as if they could read my mind. The smiles that had been on their faces all night dropped away, and the light, fun atmosphere around us became heavy and tense.

"What's up, Anna?" Marcus said.

"I *did* want to see you guys and just catch up," I said. "But there's also been something on my mind a lot lately and I can't get it out of my head. It's been, like, eating away at me."

"What is it?" Merrie said. Before I could even answer, she continued. "Nightmare Club stuff?"

I looked at her and then Marcus. I didn't say anything at first, but knew my eyes told the story without the need to say a single word.

"Yes," I said finally. When they didn't have a reply right away, I went on. "It was such a big part of our lives here. I kept it going in college kinda, but it wasn't the same. I don't know if I want to just go there and see the Dwelling once more, or, I don't know, maybe start meeting again. I'm not really sure, but I didn't want to do anything or go anywhere without talking to you guys first. Maybe," I looked around and lowered my voice, "maybe John would find a way back or something. I don't know."

For a long time neither of them said anything. We'd been back to the Dwelling after our final showdown with Mr. Nightmare. We'd talked about Chuck and John since then also, though not recently. Their reaction—or lack of reaction—was confusing.

"Come on guys, please say something?" My heart pounded hard in my chest. It could have been from the alcohol or the heat inside Guild Street Pizza, but I doubted it.

"Let's pay and talk outside, okay?" Marcus said, then grabbed for his wallet. "I've got it covered. I'll meet you outside if you want."

Merrie and I went outside, we didn't speak. What had felt like an easy, free-flowing conversation for two and a half hours with her had devolved into an awkward silence. There was a bench along the sidewalk; I pointed to it.

"Let's sit over there," I said. Merrie said nothing but followed me and we both sat on the bench. Like old times, just the two of us—the girls of the group. But not like old times because instead of friendship between us, I felt only the tension of stress and time. The things that had kept us friends but would possibly keep us from ever being as close as we once were. Thankfully, Marcus came out a few seconds later and the silence didn't have to last too long.

"Okay," Marcus said.

"Okay," I repeated. "I said what I had to say inside. You guys are my best and oldest friends. I can only talk to you two about this. I thought you would be here for me."

"We *are* here for you, Anna," Merrie said. "We'll always be here for you. Marcus and I have talked a lot about everything. We both kinda decided we wouldn't bring it up anymore. Too much…"

"But…" I tried to interrupt Merrie but she talked over me. I let her finish her thought.

"Too much happened the more we talked, right?" she said. I nodded and she continued. "So, we figured it made more sense to keep our mouths shut. Whether he's gone or not, neither of us want to go through all of the stress again. I know you don't want to, either. If we keep our mouths shut about it and never mention it again, well then, who knows, maybe less bad things will happen."

Marcus must have seen the anger on my face because before I could start in on Merrie, he jumped in.

"I know you lost more than either of us did," Marcus started.

"No fucking shit," I said. It could have been the drinks talking. I understood what they were saying. The less we talk about it, the less bad stuff could happen. I wanted to talk about it though, and these were *my* people. I could always count on them to have my back on Nightmare Club stuff. And now it was as if they were cutting me off. What else was I going to do? Who else was going to be there for me on this?

"Right," Marcus said, and put a hand on my shoulder. "None of us want to lose more. If we distance ourselves from the whole thing it might make a difference." I pushed his hand off my shoulder, then got up and stood at the edge of the sidewalk looking down the street instead of at my friends.

"We can still talk about Chuck and John," Merrie said.

I heard her and part of me wanted to turn, hug her and tell her I understood. But I was too mad. The Nightmare Club was our thing. We kept it going until I left for school. I kept it going at school—sort of—and now I was back and it was time to bring the Club back too. We had to do it for Chuck, to keep his memory alive, and for John. He needed those nightmares to live. He'd come back one day, I knew it, all we had to do was keep feeding him.

"You get it don't you? I know you're mad, but I also know you understand this," Marcus said. "We need to protect ourselves."

I did understand. My thoughts were only on Chuck and John. I needed to get out of there. More arguing would only make them want to talk more so I acquiesced to give myself a chance to leave.

"I do," I said. "I'm just upset. You guys had time to think

about it. It's all hitting me at once, I guess. It was a fun night. We should do this again, without the drama at the end." I laughed, hoping it would be enough to get them off my back.

They both looked at me, unsure.

"I'm fine, really. I get it," I said and turned to Merrie.

"Okay. Yeah, let's do this again. I'll be twenty-one in a few months then we can get drunk together," Merrie laughed. I joined her, though I think both laughs were forced—fake.

"Call either of us if you need anything," Marcus said. He was trying to take on the role of Chuck—the responsible one. He did a pretty good job, but he wasn't Chuck.

"Yeah, I will," I said. I gave Marcus a hug too.

All three of us walked into the parking lot, said one final goodbye and went to our respective cars. I got in my car and put my head on the steering wheel. It took all the effort I had not to break down into an uncontrollable fit of tears as I sat there thinking about how terribly the conversation had gone. I started the night thinking I'd be walking into the woods with my two closest friends to revisit our dark, traumatic past. Instead, I sat in my car feeling like I'd lost the only people in the world who really understood me.

I brought the Dying Buffalo to life, eased it out of the parking lot and made the quick ride home. Mom and Dad were settled in and watching TV when I got there. I said hi and then went to my room, flipped on my bedside light and grabbed a Robert McCammon paperback from my nightstand. Reading horror books pushed the horrors of the real world away. Before I got completely lost in the story, I decided tomorrow I'd visit the Dwelling by myself.

CHAPTER 3

Instead of having breakfast with Mom first thing in the morning, I woke up early, got on some workout clothes and told Mom I was going for a run. I wasn't in the same kind of shape I'd been in playing basketball or softball back in high school, but I could still run for distance, and when I did, I always felt better. That morning though, I wasn't going for a run. I was going someplace else instead.

I left the house, went down to the end of the street and walked through the neighborhood toward Red Bird Lane. It was impossible not to think about the five of us: Chuck, John, Merrie, Marcus and me, making the walk along those same streets at night. I could recall the conversations, the jokes, the dumb stuff we did as kids when we took those steps. I never took those steps alone as a kid. Usually, it was all five of us—the whole Club—though there was one time it was just Merrie and me. Yet there I was, a twenty-one-year-old adult making the walk and taking those same steps and I was by myself. At the end of Red Bird Lane, I stopped. Nothing was in front of me except the woods. I could still turn back if I wanted to. I had no intention of backing out. I had to see it again. I had to find the

Dwelling, sit there and remember. Maybe John would stop by for a visit.

I shook my head, pushing memories away, then stepped up over the curb and entered the woods.

I wasn't sure I'd get there. The place had changed in four-plus years, but once the woods surrounded me completely, I knew the way. As if a magnet was pulling me to the spot I wanted to be. I weaved between and around trees knowing exactly which path to follow until I found it. It looked pretty much the same as it did the last time I was there. A large metal drum sitting in the center of a semi-circle of fallen logs, the trees Mr. Nightmare had knocked down littered the area but the basic shape of the Dwelling was the same as it had always been. Even Mr. Nightmare couldn't destroy it. The grass and leaves were trampled flat under my feet. It brought back a memory of Chuck telling me about high school kids going out there to drink and smoke and have sex. Back then I didn't realize kids would do that stuff, but now it seemed obvious they had been partying at the Dwelling since we stopped going there and they would continue to until I had kids old enough to go there at night.

It was hot and humid. I was sweating from the walk, but the air around the Dwelling was different. It was cooler there. Dryer. As if there was a bubble around it keeping the warm, sticky air out. I circled the metal drum, looking inside to see the charred pieces of wood, and then sat down on one of the logs. I didn't sit at just any spot on the logs, though, it was *my* spot. The place I'd sat for every meeting of the Nightmare Club. I could look next to me and behind me and almost see my friends sitting in *their* spots, too. This was our place. Even though we weren't all around anymore, I could feel the five of us there, in that place.

For a while I sat there and it was as if the world disappeared around me. The forest felt as if it came in and held itself against me, hugging me when there was no brother or friends to do it for me. I sat there and breathed the summer air, enjoyed the stillness around me. It was peaceful.

From behind me a sound broke the silence—ended the peacefulness.

My eyes snapped open. Was it a squirrel running across small twigs? A bird flying down from above and landing on the piled-up dirt and leaves? It could have been, but I didn't think it was. I looked around, saw nothing, and stood up. My heart skipped for a second, my stomach dropped.

"John?" I said. I didn't yell out into the woods, but it wasn't a soft whisper either.

Wind gusted in my face and the air swirled above me. I looked up, remembering branches falling at us from above when we killed Mr. Nightmare.

"John," I said again and got up, my heart beating a little faster. Did I really think it was him, or was I hoping it was? I couldn't say. But I called him two more times and there was still no answer. I took a few steps away from the barrel and scanned the woods. Nothing there either. The wind still blew and swirled, but it did that on its own sometimes, it didn't mean there was some other worldly being there—John, Mr. Nightmare, or anything else.

I exhaled. Horror books at the time would say I let out a breath I didn't know I was holding, but I knew I was holding it. In my head, I explained everything away—even though it was weird that the wind picked up when the air had been so still before. Even though there, in the Dwelling, very little ever made sense, I was still able to rationalize what I saw. The wind was just the wind, sounds were normal sounds of the woods. I wanted to see John again. Because of the events that happened there, I knew there was more going on in the world than what most people saw. I was also an adult and I knew sometimes scary shit was your head playing tricks on you. Maybe Marcus and Merrie were right. We'd been through enough. My parents had been through enough. If John wanted to find me, he could do it on his own, he didn't need me to come looking for him. It was safer to do things the way my friends had done. It happened and now it was time to move on and try not to bring it up. I began the walk out of the woods and back home, thinking maybe I would go for a run after all—it might clear my thoughts. In my head, I told myself it would be the last time I visited. Like Merrie and Marcus had done, I decided to leave that part of my life behind. Chuck was my brother and I'd known John long before we started the Nightmare Club; I could remember them without remembering everything that had happened.

As I turned back for one final look at the Dwelling, I thought I saw a shadow move out of the corner of my eye. My heart jumped and I looked to my right. A branch wobbled back and forth with a squirrel sitting on the end of it. It was just in my head so I left, with plans to go for a run and then call Merrie and Marcus later on and tell them they were probably right about everything.

Chapter 4

I ended up running what would become my normal loop. It was about three miles; I'd taken the car out one day and figured the mileage of the different loops I ran so I knew how far I was running. No one was home when I got there so I took a shower and checked the paper for jobs again. Teaching jobs were always at the top of my list, but I was also on the lookout for bartending or waitressing jobs, because it was something I could do most nights, even if I had a teaching job when fall rolled around. After checking the paper and making a few unfruitful calls about various openings, I went into my room, laid down in bed, and grabbed my McCammon book again. I read about forty pages and felt my eyes start to close on me, so I put the book down and allowed myself to sleep.

I didn't know how long I was out but I woke up to the sound of voices. Actually, one voice in particular.

"Anna-banana," the voice said. It was soft and low, like the wind outside my bedroom window. Barely audible. In fact, it was so low and so quiet that at first I didn't know if it was really a voice or just the wind, my mind tricking me into thinking it was actually saying words. Still, I sat up, blinked a few times and looked around my room. My book was on my nightstand—bookmark placed neatly about three quarters of the way through the book. The sun was still out, so I hadn't slept long and the house seemed quiet, so Mom and Dad weren't home yet. The words were so soft and gentle, like the sound of a single beat of a butterfly's wings, they didn't register right away. I was still half asleep, trying to figure out what was going on. Then the realization of the words hit me. *Anna-banana.* There was only one person who called me that name.

I got up from my bed and looked around the room, recalling Mr. Nightmare's ability to appear out of nowhere. John was one of *them* now, a nightmare-person; maybe he could materialize in the same manner.

"John?" I whispered into the empty room. For the second time that day, I hoped I'd have the chance to see my old friend. I almost had myself convinced what I'd heard was the tail-end of whatever I'd been dreaming about during my short cat nap, when the wind spoke a second time.

"Anna-banana." It was stronger this time, louder. I could *hear* it. The words were there. I wasn't sleeping or dreaming. It was John's voice and he was asking for me, talking to me.

"John?" I said again, with more urgency in my voice this time. I needed him to know I could hear him. Mr. Nightmare told us he needed to collect enough dreams and be strong enough to enter into our world. Maybe John wasn't quite strong enough to break the wall into our world physically, but he could break through with his words alone. "John, I can hear you."

Then I was quiet. I didn't move. I didn't even breathe. I stood there and listened. If there was a message coming like the wind again, I needed to be able to hear it. So, I waited. I knew he'd answer me. I waited. Nothing. For a long time, there was only silence. I worried I'd lost him. He couldn't break through for more than a word at a time and I'd have to wait for him to recharge and eat more dreams to hear from him again. I'd given up hope completely when the wind spoke a third time.

"Anna, help," the wind said.

"John, I will. You know I will. How can I help you?" I didn't move, waiting for another reply. The wind—the real wind—outside my window stopped. I remained motionless so I wouldn't miss the next message from John. Five minutes stretched into ten and then twenty. After twenty-five minutes I finally gave up hope. There were going to be no more messages. I was excited, and the first thing I did was run into the kitchen to get the cordless phone off its base and call Merrie. I was halfway through dialing her number when I stopped. She didn't want to hear about this stuff. And the more distance I had from the event—from hearing those words—the less certain I was that it really had been John's voice. It was possible it was him, but it was also likely it was all in my head. What was happening to me? I'd been home for winter and spring break without these kinds of things happening. And I'd spent whole summers at my parents' house where my mind wasn't focused on John and Chuck. What was different about this time?

I didn't have answers, but the fact that I was so focused on them made me question what I had heard with a renewed vigor. Instead of calling Merrie, I went to Dad's liquor cabinet and grabbed his bottle of bourbon. I didn't think it was one of the expensive bottles, but I couldn't be certain. I was a twenty-one-year-old just graduating college, my idea of expensive booze was a case of Bud Light instead of a case of Red Dog. I was a college weekend drinker, and not much else. I drank as a way to have fun with my friends and loosen up a bit. Never in my life had I reached for a drink when things were difficult to deal with. But I was struggling. I missed my brother and my friend. I'd tried to talk to my friends about it, but they wanted to ignore it instead. Maybe, I thought, the bourbon would help take the edge off a little bit. It wasn't like I was doing anything bad. I was of legal age and people had a drink to ease their nerves all the time. I had willpower. If every time things got hard I reached for a bottle of booze, it would be a different story. This wasn't every time, this was *one* time. So, I grabbed a glass from the cabinet, filled it about halfway with the amber liquid, and took a sip. It burned my mouth and warmed my stomach. I exhaled, my breath tasting woody and nutty at the same time. I sat at the table—in Chuck's chair—and had a few more sips. When the glass was empty, I was starting to feel a little better. The alcohol dulled the thoughts in my head enough to let me push them to the side.

I rinsed the glass off in the sink and went to my room.

I stayed there the rest of the day.

CHAPTER 5

The next day I woke up early and was ready—if needed—to push the thoughts of Chuck and John and the Nightmare Club from my mind without the help of Dad's bourbon. Merrie and Marcus had done it; they didn't even talk about it anymore. If they could do it, so could I. I took another morning run and decided as long as I didn't have a job, I was going to keep active by running every day even if the weather was bad. I brought money with me and switched my route up so I could run past the store on the way home. Sweating and out of breath, I bought a newspaper and finished my run with the paper tucked under my arm.

There were no teaching jobs posted but there was a bartending job at a restaurant not far from my house. I called immediately and it turned out the manager was someone I knew. I'd played basketball with his daughter, Jenn, all through high school. She was bartending full time and they were looking for a second person to work with her. He hired me without even having me come in, and was excited for me to start. So was I. I'd been sitting at home reading horror books for too long. If I had more going on to occupy my mind, I might be able to get it off of the Nightmare Club and all of the hurt and pain thinking about it caused. He asked me if I could come in later that day to fill out forms and sign an official document to say I was hired. Of course, I said I'd be there.

At around one that afternoon, I hopped in the Dying Buffalo and made the fifteen-minute drive to Pete and Mary's Bar and Grill. I'd eaten there once before but didn't realize I knew the family who owned it. I'd actually met "Pete and Mary" a handful of times; they were Jenn's grandparents.

"Anna," Jenn's dad, Mr. Thornton, said when I walked in through the front door. The place was open, but there were only a few patrons inside.

"Hi, Mr. Thornton," I said and greeted him with a hug. "I knew Jenn had a restaurant in her family, but I didn't know it was this place."

"You can call me Jim when we're working, Anna," he said. "Even Jenn calls me Jim. My father always ran the place and I did my own thing back when you girls were younger. My dad's getting older, and we figured we needed more family to get involved. My cousin is a chef and he runs the kitchen. I just started taking over out here. But yeah, we never had family work here before, so this is new for all of us."

"Awesome. I'm so glad I saw your ad in the paper today." I glanced over at the bar to see if Jenn was there. I hadn't seen her in a few years.

"Jenn comes in later," Jim said. "Let's go over here and talk and get all this stuff worked out."

We talked for nearly an hour about the job and what would be expected of me. I'd never bartended before, but I'd waited tables and had a little experience mixing drinks. He said he would start me on a Monday night with Jenn so I'd be able to get some days working when it was slow, before the busy Thursday, Friday, Saturday crowd came in. The place was closed on Sunday. I signed all the papers I needed to sign, and he told me I'd start the following Monday. Before I left Jim gave me a big book of different cocktails. There was another one they kept under the bar. Some of the more popular ones were high-lighted. He didn't expect me to memorize the whole thing, but wanted me to at least be familiar with the more popular options.

I left an hour after I got there, excited to get started in a few days.

My first thought was to go home and celebrate—maybe another glass of Dad's bourbon was in order. Then I thought I'd go home and call Merrie or Marcus so I didn't have to celebrate by myself, but I wasn't sure I wanted to talk to them and it was unclear if they wanted to see me. There was a third choice—a trip to the library to return my book and pick out a new one.

I decided to go with a combination of choice number three and choice number one. I'd stop at the library, return the book I'd just finished, get a new book then go home and celebrate with a drink. Maybe Mom and Dad would be home when I got there so I wouldn't have to celebrate—and drink—alone.

Being an English and literature major in college made me read more than I even thought possible. I could read twenty-five or thirty books in a semester, depending on the classes I was taking. Being in the Nightmare Club made me want to know more about how to tell a scary story. Needless to say, when I could pick my own books to read, most of them were horror books. I would read new ones from Little, Laymon, and King when they came out, but I'd also read older stuff from the '70s and '80s. I wanted to know everything there was to know. It started as a way for me to get better at telling my own scary stories and quickly turned into an obsession. Reading scary books had become a part of who I was.

When I got to the library—the massive building used to intimidate me when I was a kid—I dropped off my book in the return slot and then looked through the new arrivals. When nothing caught my eye, I went to the horror paperback section. There wasn't a horror hardcover section like there was for mystery or science-fiction, but I liked reading the smaller paperbacks. They were easier to carry around. After a few minutes of searching, I found a book by Clive Barker I hadn't read before —The Damnation Game. He'd written a few of my favorites, so I took it with me and checked out. I loved the library now that I wasn't so small inside the huge building; being around all those books made me feel safe and curious about all the things I didn't know yet. Because being there brought so much joy, I didn't check out more than one book at a time. If I had to come back for a new book in a day or two, it was a good thing.

When I got home it was late afternoon. Mom's car was in the driveway but Dad's wasn't. Mom never drank much, but maybe she'd celebrate my job with me anyway. I tucked the library book and the book of cocktails under my arm and went inside.

"Hey, Mom," I said upon entering. I could hear her moving around in her bedroom.

"Hi, Anna," she called. I set my books on the kitchen table and waited until she came down the hall from her room.

"What have you been up to today?" Mom said as she walked into the kitchen.

"Oh, not much," I said, playing coy. "I went to the library for a new book." I held up the library book, keeping the cocktail book hidden behind it. Then I moved it out of the way really fast so she could see what was underneath. "And I got a job!"

Mom's face brightened and a smile crossed her mouth. She put her arms up and came closer to give me a hug.

"Oh, honey, that's so great. What is the job, bartending?" she asked, looking at the book I was still holding.

"Yeah, not teaching, but it's something to do for the summer and it's mostly nights anyway, so I could get a teaching job and still bartend if it ends up being a good job." I put the book down and sat back in a kitchen chair, already thinking about a celebratory drink with Mom.

"Where is it?" she asked.

I filled her in on the details about Jenn Thornton and her

family's restaurant. Turned out, Mom knew they had taken over running the place but didn't think they were hiring.

"I start next week," I said. Then, "I think we need to have a drink to celebrate. What do you say?"

"Let's do it!" Mom said, and I smiled. Glad she wasn't going to make me drink alone in the middle of the afternoon. She protested a little when I grabbed Dad's good stuff, but after I made her a rum and Coke—practicing for when I would start mixing drinks for real—she seemed okay with it. I poured Dad's good bourbon on a pile of ice cubes and drank it down. We had another drink when Dad got home. We ate dinner together and Mom went to bed shortly after. Dad and I ended up on the back porch, each of us with another glass of his good stuff in hand. We talked for a while—thankfully it was nothing heavy—and I could tell he was happy. Happy for me and happy that things had worked out okay. When Chuck passed and then John disappeared, things had teetered for a while. Mom wasn't okay and neither was I; Dad might have hidden it, but he struggled too. I'm sure there were times when we all questioned whether or not we'd make it through everything as a family. But that night felt like one of those nights you could look back on in ten or fifteen years and say, "remember when…." A few times when we were talking, I thought I heard the wind call my name. I knew it couldn't be John—it wasn't possible—so I took another drink and the sound went away. Eventually, I went to bed and passed out.

Chapter 6

The rest of the week passed in a blur. Each day I woke up and went for a run. When I got home, I showered and spent time in my room or on the back porch looking through the cocktail book, trying to learn the most popular drinks and taking a look at everything else in there so I was at least familiar with most of them. If I was outside, the wind would talk to me. It might have been John, but I could never see him, so I convinced myself it wasn't. More than once I would take a few swallows of Dad's bourbon to take the edge off and mute the voice in the wind. It usually helped and it let me get through the day. It wasn't a habit, but it was getting there.

Luckily, I started the job at Pete and Mary's Bar and Grill and it was busy enough there that I barely noticed the sound of the wind and was able to ignore it without the help of alcohol. Bartending, I was surprised to find out, was natural for me. It wasn't hard to be polite to customers most of the time—although there were some people I was nice to who didn't deserve it, but it was all part of the job. Most people ordered beer or wine or simple mixed drinks with one liquor and a soda of some sort—nothing too difficult to mix. If someone ordered a drink I didn't know, Jenn would help me out, but the more days I worked, the more confident I became making those fancy drinks. Speaking of Jenn, she and I became close again; after a few days it felt as though we hadn't spent the last four years not talking to one another.

By the middle of summer, we had a good rotation down. It was just the two of us—sometimes her father would fill in, and we worked together four days a week with one of us taking Monday off and the other taking Tuesday off, so whenever the place was open one of us was always there. We quickly became close because we spent so much time together and we had the previous friendship to build upon. Because most of the work happened in the afternoons and nights, I was still able to run every day, and I got in the best shape of my life. Once I fell into a good routine, I didn't have time to think about the fact that I hadn't talked to Merrie or Marcus in almost five weeks. And I hadn't heard the wind call me in almost the same amount of time.

Jenn was a smoker, and even though I didn't smoke, I still needed to unwind after work, so we'd sit out back after our shift ended—sometimes with her cousin, the chef and a few of the cooks—and talk. One night in late July we went out back and no one else was there with us.

"That was a pretty tame shift for a Saturday," Jenn said as she blew smoke out her nose. No doubt she was remembering the Saturday before, when we had to kick two guys out of the bar and ended up calling the cops.

"Must be because word got out that we don't take shit from these drunk assholes," I said and laughed.

"Hey," Jenn said. "I meant to tell you but just forgot, your friends Merrie and Marcus came in on Tuesday this week. They were asking for you."

"Really?" I said. My heart dropped like when you see an ex that you'd rather never run into again.

"Yeah, they said they heard you were working here now and

came in to say hi. I thought you guys were, like, super tight. You don't talk to them anymore?"

"It's kind of a long story." I kicked a rock at my feet; it rolled across the pavement, hit the wall of the restaurant and then ricocheted back toward me. "We used to be a lot closer. It's not like we're *not* friends. We're just not as close as we used to be. Merrie still lives in Prairie View; Marcus has an apartment across town. Did they say what they wanted?"

"No," Jenn shook her head. "Just that they wanted to see you and hoped they could catch you. I gave them your schedule, maybe they'll be back around this week or something."

I sighed. With Merrie and Marcus not talking to me for over a month and my friends from college strewn across the country, living and working in various cities, Jenn was now my closest friend. My relationship with Merrie and Marcus was something I'd been struggling with since the last time I saw them, and I hadn't been able to tell anyone. Telling them would require them knowing about everything that happened to lead Merrie, Marcus, and myself to this point in our relationship. Even though I wanted to fill her in, I couldn't tell Jenn most of the story. Instead, I got as close to the truth as I could.

"It was hard after Chuck died, for all of us. Marcus, Merrie, John and I, we were always together—Chuck too. After what happened to Chuck and then…John…" I stopped and took a deep breath. I hadn't talked about this much since freshman year of college. It was hard enough to process when it happened. I didn't share the story with many people anymore. Jenn must have sensed my frustration.

"You don't have to tell me if you don't want to. I get it. A lot of shit happened to you."

"No, it's okay," I said and powered onward, still being as honest as I could. "Chuck died and then John went missing, or whatever. It was really hard for the three of us. We were there for each other, but every time it was the three of us together it just felt…incomplete. I guess we could have dealt with it together. We felt the difference and the emptiness, and eventually we stopped hanging out together so much. If I was with Merrie it would be fine, or just with Marcus, it was fine. Or the two of them without me, even. Then it was fine. But when we were all together it was like two people were missing. It was easier for me to not see them than it was to deal with the problem, so that's what I did. Once I was in college it was even easier to avoid them. We got together earlier this summer but I haven't talked to them since."

"Makes sense," Jenn said and then sucked on her cigarette. "They never found out what happened to him right? The cops, I mean."

"No," I shook my head, knowing the big lie was coming. "Not knowing makes it harder. Because literally anything could have happened to him. The police said he probably killed himself because of Chuck. I don't believe that though."

"Must be hard." Jenn pulled smoke into her lungs once more and blew it out, then put her hand on my back.

"I had a huge crush on him, you know?" I had no idea where the words were coming from, but they rushed out and I felt like it wasn't the end.

"John?" Jenn said, smiling.

"Yep, good old teenage crush," I laughed.

"I get it," she said. "You guys were together so much, it's only natural."

"Even more than most people saw." Oh, shit. I was actually going to tell her this. I needed to make sure I didn't say too much, but it all spilled out anyway. "Jenn, there aren't many people that know what I'm about to tell you."

"Okay." She looked around then reached into her pocket and pulled out her pack of cigarettes. She offered one to me, like she did every time, and I declined.

"We had this club growing up." I laughed and then launched into the story. "Chuck, Marcus, Merrie, John and I. We called it the Nightmare Club. Every Saturday night after our parents were asleep, we'd sneak out into the woods and tell scary stories. One story every week and we kept score to see who produced the most nightmares."

"Wow," Jenn said. "I had no idea."

"We kept it secret on purpose." Telling her about it became easier. "We did it for, like, two years, maybe more. When Chuck died and John went missing we stopped for a while, then started again with a few other kids—younger kids. Eventually we stopped. I don't know if the club was what kept us so close and now that we're older it doesn't make much sense for us to hang out together or do other things. I don't know. Not really sure why I'm making you listen to all of this."

"It's fine." Jenn put a hand on my shoulder again. "Once you left here and went to school you put one part of your life behind you. There's a lot of bad stuff there. Before, you'd come home for a visit, but always knew you'd be leaving to go back to school. Now that chance is gone. You have a job here. Who knows how long you'll be here, so you're thinking about it more."

"Makes sense," I said.

"Yeah, if you're avoiding them because it reminds you of the bad stuff, I get it. But you should talk to them. I'm your friend and I'll help you. But the more help you have, the better."

"You're right," I said. "Thanks, Jenn." We hugged and went back inside. There was still about an hour's worth of work cleaning up the bar, it would be another late night. I got home around two in the morning—normal for the nights I worked with Jenn. I sneaked into the house quietly, even though the Dying Buffalo probably woke up the entire neighborhood. Then I took a quick shower and fell into bed. Before I fell asleep, I was certain I heard the wind talk to me.

CHAPTER 7

When I woke up the next morning, I remembered my dreams vividly. I'd dreamed of the talking wind, of John calling me in the night and asking me to help him. The conversation with Jenn about the Nightmare Club was enough to bring those thoughts back with a vengeance. I pushed them away. The last thing I wanted to do was get caught letting those intrusive thoughts invade my head again. I got dressed, grabbed my Walkman, checked the tape inside, and left the house for a run.

Whenever I ran in the past, before the first half of that summer, it was always for a purpose. I ran to get in shape for basketball season or softball season. I never ran just to run. That summer I ran to stay in shape but for nothing in particular. I wasn't playing any sports, but still, I woke up every day and felt lost if I didn't run shortly thereafter. It became as much a part of my life as eating or breathing. At the end of the school year, I'd made a mixed tape to listen to in my dorm room when drinking with my friends. I loved all the songs and thought it would make a good running soundtrack, so every day I rewound the tape to the beginning of one side and I knew I could listen without having to flip the tape until after the run was over.

After ten minutes of stretching in the front yard, I made sure my hair was pulled back tight enough to stay out of my face and began my jog. I had a few different loops by mid-summer and was feeling good, so I decided to go with the long loop, which was around six miles. Within five minutes I hit my groove. The music played in my ears, but it was just noise. I focused on keeping my pace smooth and even and maintaining slow steady breaths as I continued forward. This was when my thoughts tended to drift. When I first started bartending, I'd go through different drinks in my head while I ran. Sometimes I thought about what I'd do if I was able to find a teaching job and how I would set up my classroom. A couple times I thought about cute guys at the bar the night before. But that day when I ran, I couldn't stop thinking about Merrie and Marcus. They'd come looking for me. I didn't think they'd called. There were never any messages on the machine or passed along by Mom or Dad. As I made the last turn and headed toward home, I decided I'd give Merrie and Marcus a call when I got home. And if I couldn't get ahold of them, I'd keep trying until I did.

I stopped running at our driveway. A full six miles, plus a little extra. It was hot and I was dripping sweat. I pulled up the bottom of my T-shirt and used it to wipe the sweat off my face. The hose was on the side of the house and I usually grabbed a drink from it after a run, so I went over and turned it on, letting the water run a bit first to make sure it was nice and cold. Then I drank and let some of the spray hit my head and drip down my face and back, cooling me off. I sat on the grass and stretched, then paced around until my breathing normalized. After a second drink from the hose, I went inside to shower.

Once showered, I got something to eat and took the cordless phone from the kitchen and went out onto the back porch—the signal was strong enough to reach back there as long as you didn't wander too far from the base. Marcus worked regular weekday hours and, since it was Sunday morning, there was a good chance he was home. Merrie's hours at the nursing home were all over the place, so there was no telling when she'd be home. I decided to call Marcus first.

The phone rang three times and for a moment I thought he wasn't home and didn't have his answering machine on, but on the fourth ring Marcus picked up.

"Hello?" His voice was low and raspy. I didn't think it was possible for someone to still be in bed at this hour.

"Hey, Marcus?" I said, expecting him to recognize my voice right away. He did.

"Anna?" He was immediately more alert, more awake. There was another voice in the background. Maybe I'd woken up more than one person.

"Yep," I said. "I didn't wake you up, did I?"

"Well," he said. It was all he needed to say.

"Sorry." I sat on one of chairs on the back porch and held the phone to my ear. "My friend Jenn said you and Merrie stopped in looking for me the other day."

"Yeah, we did actually," he said. Then after a brief pause, he continued. "Merrie is actually here right now. Do you want to come over or meet somewhere?"

I laughed. I couldn't help it. I wasn't laughing at them. I thought they were always a great couple and I liked when they were together, so knowing they were together made me happy —again it might have reminded me of old times, but it still made me happy.

"You guys are awesome," I said, in case it wasn't clear I was happy for them. "I don't know where you live, though. I know you told me, but I don't know exactly where it is."

Marcus gave me directions to his place and told me where to park so I could find it. It wasn't too far away. I had already showered and was ready to go, so I fired up the Dying Buffalo and made my way across town.

When I got to Marcus's apartment building, I pulled into the parking lot, found a spot and headed toward the door of the building. Marcus had said he would buzz me in, but when I walked up, Merrie was there holding the door open for me.

"We heard you pull in." She looked over my shoulder at the Buffalo, still clicking in the parking spot.

I didn't say anything. Instead, I gave her a wide, toothy grin. It had always been our way of teasing the other without having to actually say anything.

"What?" Merrie said. "It's not the first time I've slept here."

"But it's the first time you've invited me over after," I said.

"True," she said.

"Well, I hope it works out this time." I let her walk past me to lead to way to Marcus's unit.

"Me too. But come on, there's a lot to talk about." Merrie grinned back at me. It was like everything was back to normal again.

She led me down a hallway. It wasn't the nicest apartment building I'd been in, but it wasn't the worst either. More than I expected from someone our age. Marcus must have been making pretty decent money. We went up a set of stairs, around a corner, then Merrie opened the door at the end of the hall and led us into Marcus's apartment. The inside—like the rest of the building—was nicer than expected. Marcus was in the kitchen getting coffee from his coffeemaker.

"Hey, look at you, making coffee like a real adult," I said. "More than I can say for myself most days."

He laughed. "Hey yourself, Anna. You want a coffee?" I nodded and Marcus's face got serious. I looked to Merrie and her face was serious too.

"Sure. What's up, guys?" I asked.

"Anna, we've been hearing John calling us," Merrie said.

It's a good thing Marcus hadn't given me that cup of coffee yet, because I would have dropped it on the floor.

CHAPTER 8

At first, I had a hard time believing what they'd told me. There was a long silence as the words processed in my head. I'd been living under the assumption that every time I heard the wind talk to me—call to me—it was nothing more than my mind making me hear what I wanted to hear. This changed everything. If Marcus and Merrie were hearing him too, it meant so much more. It meant he was there, really there all those times. And I'd heard him call for help. He needed help, and I'd been ignoring him.

"What do you mean?" I said once I calmed down enough to be able to talk. I'd taken a seat at Marcus's small wooden kitchen table.

"We've heard him. Like, actually heard him. Just the last few weeks." Merrie sat across from me and grabbed my hand. "I heard him a few weeks ago, but I thought it was in my head."

"Me too," Marcus chimed in. "Turned out we both heard him on the same day. He was like…"

"Calling you and asking for help," I interrupted Marcus.

"Oh shit, you too?" Marcus said.

"I thought it was in my head too. It caused a little bit of a drinking problem for a few weeks." I shrugged. "How did you figure it out?"

"We were together," Merrie said. Her cheeks got red. "And we both heard him at the same time. That's when we realized it was a real thing."

"Shit," I said.

"Anna, sorry about the way things ended last time. We should have…" Marcus started, but I interrupted him a second time. My thoughts were already going a mile a minute. I wasn't even really hearing what he was saying. I was on to the next thing we had to do.

"Well, then, listen. He needs our help, right? You heard him say that?" I asked. They both agreed, and I kept talking. I reminded myself of John when he spoke too fast because he was excited about something. "He needs dreams—nightmares—to get stronger. We know that already. It's one of the few things we know from Mr. Nightmare or John, or whoever told us about it originally, I don't remember. The point is, he has to feed on them so he can come here. The reason his voice is so faint and we can barely hear it is because he doesn't have enough dreams to come through and fully talk to us and communicate with us. It has to be the reason he's trying to get our attention."

"We don't know for sure, but we guessed the same thing, too," Marcus said.

"So, let's go out to the fucking woods and do this. Let's make some nightmares for him." I stood up, ready to go out to the Dwelling. Neither Marcus nor Merrie stood up. "What, you guys already talked about this, huh? You figured I'd want to do something crazy when I found out."

"Well, kinda." Merrie pulled at my hand until I sat back down. "We want to help him. But we want to find out more first. There's no way to know if going out there and telling stories will actually help him or not. We only *know* that he wants our help. The rest is just a guess. We figured if the three of us stayed together and we could all hear him at the same time, maybe we can talk to him and find out how to really help him instead of just guessing."

She was right and I knew it. I hated it, but we didn't need to go out into the woods to tell scary stories. We weren't kids anymore, we could control things better at Marcus's place or wherever we wanted to try to make contact with John. Arguing with them about running off into the woods wouldn't help John any more or any less. It was something to do, a way to get out nervous energy. The smart thing to do was to stay and wait for John to make contact with us again. If we were ready for it we could ask him what he needed from us. Doing anything else was just making wild assumptions.

"You're right," I said.

"Looks like you got your wish," Marcus said.

"What's that?" I said.

"Nightmare Club reunion," he laughed, and it broke the tension. It took a little over a month, but he was right. We were back together.

John had disappeared in the Dwelling following our confrontation with Mr. Nightmare, but he'd popped up here and there for years after. It was nice knowing he was around. Then, one day, he stopped popping up. He didn't appear to any of us after that; he was gone. Before his sudden disappearance, he'd been angrier when he made those random appearances, as if being in the land of Nightmares—the Nightmare Realm as he called it—had changed him. As it would change anyone. He never explained what it was like there, only saying it was different than here. Then one day his visits stopped. In all that time, I never stopped thinking about him. He was always there in the back of my mind. And now he was back—sort of.

"How did it start for you?" Merrie said while we sat at the table. It was not even noon yet, but Marcus got beers out of the fridge. I drank down half a can in two quick gulps and then told them my story of hearing John calling me in the wind. I left no detail out, telling them everything, from our dinner at the pizzeria to sitting there at Marcus's kitchen table. I tried to include my thoughts and what I was feeling—even when those thoughts were about the two of them—some of it was hard to talk about, but they deserved to hear the unedited truth.

Merrie and Marcus each gave me a story which was similar to mine. They heard John calling them and assumed they were imagining things, until they'd been laying in Marcus's bed quietly and heard him at the same time. They even included the bits about how they were able to rekindle their romantic relationship, which they didn't have to do. I didn't need to hear it, but it was fun to learn all the little details.

"And then you both realized when you heard the same thing that it wasn't just in your head," I said, stating the obvious.

"Yep," Marcus said. "We called you right away; your mom said you were at work. We went over there the next night but you were off."

"Makes sense," I said. "What do we do now?"

Merrie shrugged. "I think we have to wait around and try to talk to him. Since we've all been ignoring him all this time."

We finished our beers and ate some lunch. We spent the whole rest of the day there. Once again, we fell right back into our old roles. It was like we hadn't missed a beat and the conversation we had outside of the pizzeria never happened. Unlike last time, we talked about Chuck and John, we talked about the Nightmare Club, we even talked—openly—about Mr. Nightmare. It was a strange, though not unwelcome, discussion. It got to be late. It was Sunday so the restaurant wasn't open, but I was getting tired.

"You remember sitting around John's basement waiting for Mr. Nightmare?" Marcus said. My eyes fluttered back open as and I sat up straight on his couch.

"How could I forget that night?" I said.

"I was so pissed at you, Anna," Merrie said with a smile.

"You were. I deserved it, though," I said. I opened my

mouth to talk again when the wind gusted hard outside. Even though Marcus had the windows shut and his air conditioner on, the wind felt like it came into the apartment somehow, like it had passed through the windows and was inside with us.

And then it spoke to us.

"Guys, help," the wind said. It was John's voice. I could picture him there with us. I sat up and glanced from one corner of the apartment to the other. Merrie and John did too, all of us coming to attention, our ears and eyes alert for our old friend.

"John!" Marcus said. "Where are you? Can you see us?"

I stood up, but I didn't want to breathe, I didn't want to move the air around us, afraid any disruption of the delicate atmosphere would cause a ripple and make John disappear from our world once again.

"Yes, I'm here. Not strong enough to come through. Need help," he said. The words were no more than a whisper, if I breathed too hard I wouldn't have been able to hear him. They were scrambled, like talking to someone on a walkie-talkie that was almost out of range. The words came at different volumes and sometimes cut out completely.

"How can we help?" I blurted.

"More dreams," John said. "He has us trapped, Anna-b."

My heart dropped. I felt like I was going to puke. I knew the answer to my question before I even asked it.

"Who has you?" I said. My muscles tensed. Maybe he wasn't going to say the name, maybe it was someone else who had him trapped. I doubted it though. The looks on Merrie's and Marcus's faces told me they were expecting the same answer as me.

"You know who," John said, our old code. But then he clarified. "Mr. Nightmare."

CHAPTER 9

Ten years before, the threat of Mr. Nightmare had faded only moments before John dissolved from our world. All of us, even John, thought we'd killed him. John had taken his dreams. We heard him scream and watched him flicker out of existence. Then John disappeared as well. Mr. Nightmare would always be a part of my life; he took my brother. But I'd always assumed he was in the past. We'd killed him.

But here was John—talking to the remaining members of the Nightmare Club like some kind of whisper—telling us Mr. Nightmare wasn't just alive, but that he'd somehow trapped John. And John needed our help.

My stomach twisted into a knot. I wanted to help him, but the realization of all of this made my legs weak. I could tell Marcus and Merrie felt the same way.

"Son of a bitch," Merrie said under her breath, reminding me of the attitude she always had toward Mr. Nightmare.

"How can we help?" I said into the air, hoping John was still able to hear us.

I was met with silence. None of us breathed, none of us moved. We didn't want to miss the message. I closed my eyes and focused on the air around us, listening for John's strained, weak voice coming through. After about ten minutes, I exhaled.

"I think he's gone," I said, hoping his voice would interrupt me.

"I think so," Merrie said.

"Yeah. I can't believe this. I thought we were done with this shit." Marcus was sweating, and I thought I saw his hand tremble.

"Me too," I said.

"We can still be done," Marcus said in a low voice. His face was flat and even. There were no emotions in his words or on his face. I didn't like the look of it.

"What do you mean?" I said. I had an inkling of what he was thinking. If I was right, what he had in mind was terrible, and I wanted to make him say the words aloud as if actually speaking them would change his mind on the subject. I also didn't want to assume the worst in my friend.

"John's gone," Marcus said. There was fear in his eyes. "He's been gone into some nightmare world, or whatever he used to call it, for ten years. Who knows if we can even get to him. What can we do to help him? Have nightmares? We're not kids anymore, right? Whatever happens over there, we don't have to be a part of it."

"He gave up everything for us and you just want to leave him there, suffering or whatever is happening to him?" I said. Marcus didn't say anything and instead looked at Merrie. For a moment I thought there was a real possibility I'd be doing this on my own until Merrie spoke.

"Don't look at me," Merrie said. "I'm with Anna—and John —on this one. If he's in trouble we need to do what we can to help him. Even if it means we have to come face to face with that fucking asshole again."

Marcus turned and walked to the far end of his apartment. There was a door leading out to a small patio. He pushed the curtain to the side and looked out at the street. We were up high enough that he could see over the low trees planted around the building. Cars passed and clouds floated by slowly, the bright blue sky looking almost unreal behind them.

"I've worked so hard for this," Marcus said. He didn't turn, instead spoke to the glass. I wasn't even certain if he was talking to Merrie and I, or talking to himself. I was still angry at him, but I let him have this time. Maybe he would come to see the right side of things on his own. "Four years of college, a decent paying job making enough to get my own place. Those things don't happen on their own. My parents didn't have money to pay for college. I worked through all four years. I didn't go out drinking or to parties on Friday and Saturday nights. I just worked and saved money when I wasn't studying."

He sniffed. He might have been crying. Merrie noticed it too, and she moved to go to him. I put a hand on her arm and stopped her. Marcus was working through something, and I thought we needed to let him do it on his own. His words weren't for us.

"All I ever wanted was a place of my own. You don't know how many family members told me it wouldn't happen. I proved them all wrong," he continued. "That motherfucker killed Chuck. And we killed him. We *thought* we killed him. It would be so easy to pretend it was just the wind again. I don't hear anything. It's not John who needs help. It's the fucking wind. I could keep going to work like nothing is wrong."

He turned to face us and let the curtain fall closed behind him. His eyes were red and wet, tears dripped down his cheeks. Marcus wiped them away with the palm of his hand.

"It would be easy to do." He took a deep breath. There was a small grin on his face; in his eyes I saw the fight I'd seen in him the first time we faced Mr. Nightmare. "But it would be the wrong thing to do. I did all of those things because of what John did for us. We killed Mr. Nightmare before and we can do it again."

"Fuck yes," Merrie said. I smiled, my anger melting away. I loved the two of them like I never could any other people. We were in it together and we'd decided to take the fight to Mr. Nightmare once more. The Nightmare Club really *was* back.

CHAPTER 10

I stayed at Marcus's place that night. It was Sunday and he had to be up early in the morning for work, but we couldn't bring ourselves to split up. I called home and told Dad I'd be staying out the night and would be home in the morning. John could reach out to us again at any time, and we needed to be ready for him. Merrie and Marcus slept in his bed and I slept on the couch. It wasn't a terrible night's sleep. When Marcus came out of his bedroom in the morning, he woke me up. He said he didn't care if I kept sleeping but Merrie was awake too. I got up, but stayed out of Marcus's way so he could finish getting ready for work. Before he left, we all agreed to keep an ear out for John. If he reached out again, we needed to be ready with our questions.

When I got home Dad gave me a wave as he was pulling out of the driveway, and I waved back as I was pulling in. I had planned to get home and go for a run, but by the time I got in the house, my limbs felt like they weighed a thousand pounds each. When I saw mom watching *Good Morning America* while she had her morning coffee, I stopped and sat down on the couch to watch with her. Joan Lunden was in the middle of a cooking segment and Mom was invested in it. Once it went to commercial, she turned to me.

"You stayed out with Merrie last night?" she said.

"Yes, Merrie and Marcus, actually. We were up too late talking and drinking and figured it was smarter to stay over instead of driving," I said.

"I'm so glad you all stayed close. Even after all these years." Her mouth quivered for a second. Neither of us had to say it, but there were two people missing from our little group. It didn't matter how many years passed, Chuck—and to a lesser extent, John—was missed at our house every day. I know I wasn't the only one who thought of him whenever I looked at his chair at the table or walked by his bedroom. Mom had been a mess at first, but that was to be expected, and eventually she'd pulled herself out of it.

"We had some fun times together, and some hard times too," I said. "It brought us closer than we realized back then. Even when we went our own ways for a while. I think they will always be my best friends."

"That's a good thing. Life-long friends are great and very hard to come by. I hope you're always close, even if you don't see each other as much as you did before. Life happens, but you always have your friends," she said as the show came back on. We were both lost in our thoughts and neither of us said anything more. My eyes started to droop, and I knew I was falling asleep sitting there on the couch. I let my eyes close and the sound of the next interview lulled me to sleep.

When I woke up, *The Price is Right* was on, and Bob Barker was asking the contestant if a tube of toothpaste cost more or less than $1.67. I blinked a few times and looked around, realizing I'd slept for at least an hour and a half. I didn't hear Mom in the house, but that didn't mean she wasn't there. She'd changed the channel to CBS at some point before she left me. I sat up, pushed my hair out of my face, and squeezed my eyes closed tight again, trying to clear the fog of my mid-morning nap. My back ached; it was the second couch I'd slept on in the last eight hours.

"Anna," a voice said. I thought it was Mom calling me from the basement or the back yard because it was so soft, but I realized it wasn't her. It was the wind. It was John.

"John?"

"Anna-banana. Help me," John's voice in the wind said.

"We will John, how? Tell me how?" My heart hammered in my chest. I held my breath. I didn't want to miss what he said. The only sound was the TV. I reached over, grabbed the remote and hit mute.

"...a gate." John said. I'd missed the first part. Fucking Bob Barker.

"Say it again. Please," I said. In my head I was begging he was able to stick around long enough to repeat his message.

"There's a gate. To here. The walls are thin there," he said, his voice growing faint.

"Where? Where is the gate? We'll go there," I said. I'd fallen to my knees in the middle of the living room.

Silence. I held my breath and waited for a response. There was nothing. Then the phone rang. It pulled my attention away from John and filled the silence. Too much noise meant I couldn't get the message from John. The phone was in the kitchen. At first, I didn't move, listening for John in between the rings, but there was still nothing. I got up and sprinted out of the living room and down the hall to the kitchen. I grabbed the phone, picked it up and slammed it back down on the base. Silence filled the house again. Silence and nothing else. John was gone. He was there and the TV had ruined my chances of helping him. It was quiet until the phone rang again. I picked it up and slammed it down a second time, still listening for John's voice. The phone rang once more, and I snatched it up.

"Hello," I growled into the phone. I took a deep breath, knowing I had to be civil with whoever it was.

"Anna!" Merrie said from the other end of the phone. "I just talked to him."

"What?!" I couldn't even believe it. I almost dropped the phone but caught it and leaned my palm against the kitchen counter, my pulse throbbing against the back of my eyes.

"For real. I'm at home, but my mom is here too. We need to talk. I tried Marcus but he was working."

"Okay, I'll walk over to you. Meet me halfway?" I said.

"Yep," she said, and we both hung up.

I threw on a pair of shoes, grabbed my keys just in case, and headed out the front door. I pulled the door locked behind me, jumped down off the front porch, and headed toward Merrie's house.

CHAPTER 11

I wasn't jogging to Merrie's house, but it wasn't a lazy summer stroll either. I walked with a purpose. When we were kids, we'd always call each other and say we were going to meet halfway—usually to meet up and then go down to the Field. I didn't really know where we were going when we got together this time, but it was a nice reminder of days past. I turned the corner at the end of a street and saw Merrie coming toward me at the same brisk pace I had. We both picked up to a jog until we were together.

"I heard him too!" I said, as soon as we were within shouting distance. I explained how I hadn't been able to hear John because of the TV.

"That's crazy, it was almost at the same exact time," Merrie said.

"What did he say?" I grabbed her elbow and turned so we could walk while we talked instead of just standing at the side of the road.

We walked in step down the street with no destination in mind. I let Merrie talk.

"I was in the bathroom, and it was just quiet in there, you know?" Merrie's words came at me fast. "I've been trying to be in quiet places all morning because I felt like it would be easier to hear him, right? Anyway, I hear him call to me and I said his name. He said he didn't have a lot of time, but there's a place where we can get to where it is easier to see him or something. A thin place, he called it."

"He told me the same thing. Well, he said a gate," I said. We turned a corner and I realized we were going to walk by John's old house. His parents had moved out and two different families had lived there since, but I'd always think of it as John's house.

"Yes!" Merrie was so excited she almost hit me in the chest. "Sorry. Yes, he said a gate or a thin place. I asked him where the gate was and he said something I couldn't hear—the only word I got was 'farm.' It was quiet for a few minutes after that and I kept listening. But there was nothing else. After a few minutes I left the bathroom and called you. Mom thought I was fucking crazy running through the house to the phone, but I told her it was something I forgot to tell you," Merrie said.

We walked past John's house and we both stopped talking. I glanced over at the house, Merrie did too. Then for some reason we stopped walking. We looked at the house, and I thought about the fun times we had as a group. The hot dogs John made on the back porch and the times we walked by before heading to the Field. I also remembered the night we spent in John's basement—the night we figured out how we could kill Mr. Nightmare. I thought we were successful, but now it appeared we weren't rid of him yet.

"Come on," I said and gave Merrie's arm another little tug. "We have more work to do."

"Yeah," she said. We walked for a few minutes without saying anything, headed this time for the Field. "Anyway, to finish my story, I called you as soon as I got out of the bathroom. And you hung up on me twice. I called Marcus's office number but it went to his answering machine. I left a message for him to call me at home, then I called you back."

"It sounds like we need to be at a farm then, but we don't know where it is."

Merrie nodded and we both dropped into silent thought. We went in and around the curved roads of the Prairie View neighborhood we knew so well. Eventually the street opened up and the tall trees were behind us and we were looking out over the Field. It was the middle of the day on a Monday, so the place was crawling with kids at summer camp. The screams and shouts cut through the dry, warm air and reminded me of the way summers used to be. Even with the place seemingly covered with little kids, we would have been able to find our own little corner for ourselves.

"We need more information. Maybe he reached out to Marcus too?" Merrie said. It was her turn to grab my arm, and we walked across the street together and through the parking lot of the Field.

"I doubt it; if it's not quiet at his job then John probably assumed we'd hear him better. Or Marcus didn't even get a chance to hear him," I said.

"That makes sense," Merrie said. We stood in the parking lot for a few minutes, then she looked at me. "Are you thinking what I'm thinking?"

We didn't even have to say it aloud. We both knew where this walk was going to end up, so we turned on our heels and left. If John was going to reach out for us together, there was only one place it would happen.

We got down to the end of Redbird Drive about ten minutes later. We stepped over the curb and went into the woods, the trees closing in around us like they always did. I made the same walk I had made earlier in the summer when I had vowed never to return, but I was back. Last time it was to reminisce, this time it was with purpose.

"Should we have waited for Marcus?" I said, pushing a branch full of leaves out of my face and holding it out of the way until Merrie grabbed it, so it wouldn't whip back into her.

It was probably too late to ask the question, because we were almost there, but I'd been thinking about it.

"Maybe, but I think he'll understand. We can't wait on this, right? We have to at least try."

"Yeah," I said. "You're right. This might not even work." Even as I said the words, I didn't really believe them. The Dwelling had always held a little extra magic for us; maybe it would provide us a little bit more. If we could get in touch with John long enough for him to tell us where we needed to go—where this farm was—the magic might actually be used for good this time.

When I got to the clearing I slowed, then stopped and let Merrie come into position next to me.

"Wow," she said. "It looks pretty much the same, huh?"

"I'm sure other kids have used it for who-knows-what since it was our place, but yeah, it hasn't really changed all that much."

Merrie walked around the circle of fallen logs much like I'd done when I was there. She kicked at a few small bushes which had grown up through the dirt in places where they weren't supposed to be, as if trying to make the Dwelling match her memory of the place. After walking around the circle once, she stopped behind the moss-covered log that had been hers. She put her foot up on the log and scraped the green stuff off with the bottom of her sneaker. With a deep breath, Merrie stepped over the log and sat down in her spot.

I walked over to the spot I used to sit in every week and sat down too. We didn't say a word, we didn't have to. We were there with a purpose, so we both stopped and listened. I didn't know how Merrie thought John's voice sounded, but I was listening for the words in the wind. I kept my breathing light and shallow. All at once I realized I wasn't waiting to see if John was going to talk to us, it was more like I was expecting him to talk, like we'd made an appointment to see him.

The wait turned out to be short. Within a few minutes, the

wind began to swirl around us. I looked up; the trees above swayed back and forth in a cool breeze. I looked over at Merrie and she was looking up too. We both knew it was happening.

The wind stopped and I listened, and then it spoke.

"Anna-banana," John said.

I glanced at Merrie and looked around for John.

"I'm here, John," I said softly. I didn't want to do anything to make him go away. I didn't even want to move. "How can we help you?"

"Places where the wall between worlds is thin. Shaw's Farm. Can explain more there. Hurry. He has us." His voice was stronger, louder. Like he could have been standing right there with us. I could picture his face. Even though I knew I would never be able to see it again, it was good to imagine it. I was older, but I never stopped loving him. I wish I'd been able to hug him one last time before he left.

"We'll be there, John. We'll be there tonight," Merrie said.

"Hurry," was the response through the wind. The breeze picked up again, the trees swirled above us once more, and then the wind stopped. The air became still. He was gone. We didn't have a reason to be at the Dwelling anymore. Our work was done, and we knew what needed to happen. Without a word we got up and left. We had to get word to Marcus. We needed to get ready to go to Shaw's Farm.

CHAPTER 12

S haw's Farm was a few towns over. We'd all been there as kids. It had been the big third-grade elementary school field trip because it was an organic farm, which were few and far between in the '80s. The fields were huge and stretched for miles in every direction. I remembered turning onto one of the roads nearby while riding the school bus on our field trip. There was farmland all around us—nothing new in that part of Illinois, but when I knew those fields were part of Shaw's Farm, I assumed we were almost done sitting on the bus. I was wrong, there were still about ten minutes left of the ride before we got to the main farm area where the equipment was stored and the farmhouse sat. Before I graduated high school however, the farm had suffered a major fire—a few of the barns, some of the silos and most of the crops were destroyed. The Shaw family, who owned the place, was never able to get the farm back up and running again like the old days, and they eventually sold the land to a neighboring farm. The land was still used for crops, but the buildings, including the farmhouse where the Shaw family used to live, that survived the fire had sat untouched for the last five or six years.

When Merrie and I got back from our walk out to the

Dwelling, the first thing we did was call Marcus from my house. He was on lunch break, and we gave him the short version of what we'd found out. He couldn't—or didn't want to —take off from work early. We understood and told him we'd be there to pick him up when he was done at six.

Merrie and I were both supposed to work that night so we had calls to make. Merrie left with the promise to come back at four in the afternoon so we could collect Marcus and make our way to Shaw's Farm. We'd be there by six if not sooner.

I collapsed down on the couch, anxious for a few minutes to catch my breath.

"Anna," Mom called from the kitchen. The time I needed to collect myself wasn't meant to be.

"Hey, Mom," I said.

"Busy morning for you?" Mom said. "I thought you'd be asleep on the couch the rest of the day. You didn't even move when I left."

"You could say it's been busy, yeah," I said. It was time for the lying to start. When I was younger the lies came out so easily. Since then, I tried to keep the lying to a minimum with my parents, but it seemed to me like whenever Mr. Nightmare was involved, lying was part of the process. "I have to call out for work tonight. I have to help Merrie and Marcus with some-thing. It's kind of an emergency." Not totally a lie.

"Oh no. I hope everything is okay." Mom leaned against the wall and pushed her hair out of her face. "Anything I can do?"

"No," I said, getting up, knowing I should call Jenn as soon as possible. "I'm not sure they want me to tell people. If I can, I will though." Again, not totally a lie.

"I understand. You're a good friend." Mom stood up straight again and went back into the kitchen, I followed her.

I grabbed the phone off the base and dialed the restaurant.

"Hello, Pete and Mary's Bar and Grill," Jim said after three rings.

"Hi, Jim, its Anna," I said.

"Oh no, I know that tone of voice," he said. I could tell he was joking.

"Yeah, sorry. I have to call out tonight. I hope it's okay. It's kind of an emergency," I said.

"It's okay. Jenn is here. I'm sure she can handle it. There's no Monday Night Football yet, so it shouldn't be too busy," he said. "I hope everything's alright. Is there anything I can do?"

"Yeah. Everything should be fine after tonight. You don't have to worry about me," I said.

"Okay. Oh, here's Jenn, she wants to talk. Good luck with everything tonight," Jim said.

"Thanks," I said. There was a momentary silence then the sound of the phone being passed from one person to the next. I wasn't really looking forward to talking to Jenn. She'd want to know more than either Mom or Jim. She was going to dig for more, like a friend would. She *was* a friend and I'd probably tell her more than I told anyone else, but I hadn't had time to come up with a cover story yet so I was going to have to deflect for the time being.

"Hey," she said.

"Hey, I'm not gonna be in tonight," I said.

"I heard," she said. "Everything good?"

"Yeah, yeah. I'll tell you more next time I see you. It'll be fine."

"Okay. I'm going to hold you to that, though. I want all the details," she said. Then after a beat, "This is about your friends who came in the other night, right?"

I laughed; it couldn't be helped. She was too good at reading me, I guess. "You got it. I'll help them out and then fill you in later. Thanks for holding down the place. Don't make a mess tonight," I joked. Jenn was always making a mess under the bar and cleaning it up at the end of the night. I tried to keep everything neat so there was less work to do after the place closed. It was a difference in styles and we joked about it a lot.

JOE SCIPIONE

"I'm going to make a mess and leave it for you," she joked back. "I gotta run though. See you, Anna."

"Bye," I said and ended the call.

With work set, I grabbed a snack and ate in my room while I packed a bag of things we might need out on the abandoned farm. I didn't really know what was in store for us, so I packed a change of clothes and a few cans of soda and some granola bars. I also threw in a flashlight and a kitchen knife when Mom wasn't looking. I didn't expect to need the knife, but I figured it was better to have a weapon and not need it. I paced around the house for a little while until Merrie came and knocked on the door. She talked to Mom while I waited, trying not to look impatient. Mom was genuinely happy to see Merrie, and they ended up talking longer than expected. By the time we left, it was almost five. We got in Merrie's car and drove to the other side of town to pick up Marcus. When all three of us were in the car, Merrie and I up front and Marcus in the back seat, we took off toward the town of Jackson and Shaw's Farm.

CHAPTER 13

It was still light out as we took the right turn onto the road where Shaw's Farm was located, but the sun was starting to set, casting long shadows through the trees and making the road dark, even though the sky was still a bright blue. The last time I'd seen the farm I was struck by how green everything looked. As we approached the driveway to the old, abandoned buildings, I was amazed because it somehow looked even greener than it had the last time I saw it. The fields were still being maintained but the buildings—just barely visible above the tops of the tall corn stalks in the field to our left—were not as well off as the crops.

"You think they have cameras out here?" Marcus said as Merrie slowed the car.

"The last thing I remember hearing about cameras was that it was too expensive to run wires to watch it all," Merrie said. "Something about the fact that it would cost more to run cameras across an entire farm than they lose in crops people might try to steal, so it wasn't worth it."

"They might have people keeping an eye out though," I said. "The more we can stay out of sight, the better."

Merrie turned right, past the signs reading 'No Trespassing,' and guided the car along the narrow dirt road toward the farmhouse and the barns that survived the fire. There was a small hill that we drove up and then came down the other side and then continued toward the buildings.

"I think we're out of sight now," Marcus said from the back seat, looking behind him. I followed his gaze; the road was no longer visible behind us. Instead, I could only see the hill, a dirt road in the middle of rows and rows of corn rising up to a crest.

"That's good," Merrie said. "I'll pull around behind the farmhouse and park there so hopefully we can stay out of sight.

The corn stalks surrounded us on either side as the car slowed and we approached the buildings. When we got closer, I realized the buildings didn't just look dingier than when they'd been more properly maintained, they were actually falling apart. The wood siding was rotting and coming down in some places, and I could see inside the farmhouse around the rotting window frames. The closer silos were also in disarray. They were made of metal, and the entire first three or four feet was rusted brown and curling. The grass was overgrown like whoever maintained these field didn't do anything other than harvest the corn, leaving the grass to grow wild on its own.

Merrie rolled the car slowly around behind the farmhouse.

"Think anyone can see us here?" she asked.

"I don't think so," I said, looking around. The road was totally out of sight, and while the field stretched on behind the house and silos, there were no other buildings where someone would be watching out for trespassers. Merrie turned the car off. I reached for the door handle but before I could get out, Marcus stopped me with a hand on my shoulder.

"Listen, I know you guys probably don't want to hear this," Marcus said. "I understand wanting to help John and I'll do anything I can for him. But I can't get arrested for trespassing. You know? I have a job. Merrie, you probably can't either. I want to look out for us, too."

I knew he was going to say something like that. He'd

become the voice of reason. We never cared about the rules when we were kids, but we'd grown up; there were always consequences now. I was a little mad he thought it was okay for me to get arrested, but I let it go. Starting an argument with him then wouldn't do anything to help John, and that's why we were there. If I was still mad about it later, I could talk about it then.

"Listen," I said. "We don't know what John wants us here for. Or even if he can contact us right now. Let's do what we can for him and find out what he wants, if we can. Then we'll get out of here. If the cops come, we're old friends from high school, home for the summer. We had the best time here for a field trip when we were kids and we wanted to check the place out again. Most cops grew up around here, they came here as a field trip too, they'll understand."

"I like it," Merrie said right away.

"Yeah," Marcus said. "It's okay, I guess. I'd rather not have to deal with it at all."

"I think we all want that," Merrie said.

We got out and pushed the car doors closed quietly instead of slamming them shut. I surveyed the area and wandered over toward the farm house. I remembered going into the house as a kid, but the family lived in most of the house, so we only went into the front foyer area. Everything else was off limits. The woman who'd given us the tour explained that they lived on the farm and took care of it, and because farm work was non-stop it made sense to live where they worked. Merrie and Marcus came up behind me as I climbed up the porch stairs.

"You going in?" Merrie whispered.

"Why not?" I said. "It's a place to start. John said the curtain between worlds was here somewhere. We have to start looking and hope he knows we're here." The wood creaked as I went up the old stairs to the front door. The porch was as run down as the rest of the house. It didn't look like it had only been abandoned for a few years—it seemed more like no one had been there for decades. The wood was worn and falling apart, the tops of nails were sticking up out of the floorboards in some places, and the wood was loose and sagging under my weight in others. I recalled the porch on our field trip having hanging plants across the top, swinging in the wind. The bright white paint of the porch had become dark and gray, covered with dirt and dust and time. The front door was locked; the knob wouldn't turn in either direction. The doorjamb, though, looked as rotted as the porch so I gave it a little pull. The wood of the jamb fell to the floor and the door swung open.

I looked back at Marcus, who was right behind me, and grinned.

"Looks like we're going in." He returned the smile. It was then I knew everything would work out.

I didn't know how far from the truth I was.

CHAPTER 14

Inside the farmhouse it was more of the same. The place was mostly empty. At least the Shaw's were able to get their stuff out of the house before they left, though a few pieces of furniture remained. The floors creaked when we walked across them. While most of the downstairs was empty, the things that were there were covered in a thick layer of greenish-gray grit no doubt a combination of dirt and dust in the air as well as pollen that had found its way inside from the crops on the other side of the rotting walls.

"Should we check upstairs?" Merrie asked, putting her hand on the banister leading up to the second floor. It was starting to get darker, and while the downstairs had a lot of windows, going upstairs looked as though we would be climbing into a dark, wooden cave. I looked up there with her, and then we looked at each other and shook our heads.

"Not if we don't have to, I think." I smiled at her and she nodded.

"John," I said. I didn't quite yell, but it was louder than the whispers we'd been using since we arrived, and it sounded loud to my ears. Marcus, who had wandered to the back of the house, joined Merrie and I by the front door. After I called, we stopped moving and listened for him.

There was no answer, but still we waited.

"John." It was Marcus this time, calling to his friend, and I could feel the reservations he'd had the day before—even just driving onto the farm a few minutes before—melting away. We were together again—the three of us, plus wherever John was. We were the Nightmare Club again.

"John." Merrie was the last to call out his name. "We're here because you told us to come. What do you need from us?"

There was a squeak. All three of us looked up. Footsteps on the floor above us.

"John!" I said, moving to the stairs. With my foot on the bottom step, I looked back at my friends. They both nodded and I went up into the black cave.

There was only a single long hall at the top of the stairs with closed doors lining both sides. It stretched the length of the house. I listened and called John's name again. Another squeak from the end of the hall. I should have been scared, maybe I *was* scared, but it didn't register in the moment. It didn't hesitate or even stop to think about what I was doing. Instead, I went ahead down the hall and opened the door at the end. It didn't even occur to me that Mr. Nightmare might have been on the other side. Luckily, he wasn't.

The door opened with a squeak. The windows in the small bedroom let light in from the outside and illuminated the hall as well, making the entire upstairs feel less ominous. I entered, and while the light slipped in through the windows, it didn't reach all corners of the room. I looked around and at first didn't see anything. Merrie and Marcus moved in behind me, their hands on my back as I took a second step into the room. There was movement in one of the dark corners. I jumped and Merrie let out a quick gasp.

"Anna-banana." It was John's voice. Strong, no longer talking on the wind. He was there with us.

"John," I said, and turned to face the man in the corner, who I still couldn't see very well.

"It's me," he said. He came forward a step out of the darkness. He was taller than I remembered, though I'm sure I was too. His hair was long and hung over his face—a face that wasn't really a face at all—and he had his baseball cap pulled down low so even if I wanted to see his face, no light would shine on it.

"I'm glad you came," he said. "All of you." The more he talked the more I realized it didn't quite sound like him. It was his voice, but it was as though there were more than one of him talking at once, a cacophony of voices all speaking at the same time. Like Mr. Nightmare's voice. It was uncomfortable.

"Of course, buddy," Marcus said. He and Merrie moved all the way into the room, the three of us standing on one side, John on the other.

"I need to explain fast before he comes back," John said. He took a step toward us and I could see he wasn't all the way there. He was there in the house with us, but also not. I could see right through him to the rotting, cracked wood paneling behind him. I didn't say anything, but I kept my eyes down, watching the wall as he spoke.

"Mr. Nightmare?" Merrie said. "Let him come here, we'll fuck him up again."

John shook his head. "He's too strong to care about you now. He remembers me but I'm one of a hundred—maybe more."

"What do you mean? We thought he was dead."

"No." John sighed like he was as disappointed as we were, maybe even more so. Then he started, talking fast like he always did when he was excited, reminding me why I had a crush on him. "When he disappeared, he went back to where we are now, the Nightmare Realm. There are lots of us there, like him—like me. I guess you'd call us nightmare-people or nightmare-eaters, maybe. We survive on nightmares. That much of what he told us was true. We can come and go from this world, but only in places like this where the barrier is thin. It's where he came through back then. Once he came over through this gate, then he could move around where he wanted as long as it was close by, like how he came into my room the night after Chuck's funeral. But he had to come through here first. Now he's taken us prisoner. Chained us up. We need nightmares to live. We collect them and then he comes and takes them from us."

"The same guy we saw?" I asked.

"Yes," John said. "He is becoming more powerful every day. Enslaving more of us. He wants to control the entire Realm."

John faded until he was almost gone completely, and then came back into focus.

"I can't stay much longer," he said.

"How can we help you, then? Do you know a way we can go there?" Marcus said.

"Nightmares, I need more of them. You can't come here unless one of the nightmare people is there in your world. We are like doorways to the Realm. I think I've figured out a way to keep him from taking the dreams from me. But I need more nightmares. If I don't have to hunt for them, I might be able to stop him, or at least slow him down. Just try, okay guys? Anna-b? More nightmares. I don't know, tell stories again or something."

"Yeah," I said. "Of course, we'll try. We'll come up with something."

"Thanks. I'll call to you again. Can you come here once in a while? Call me. I will hear you."

We nodded.

"It's good to see you. Nightmare Club is looking good," he said. I could tell he was smiling—or at least smirking under his hat and all that hair.

"You too, John," Marcus said.

"Talk soon," he said. He faded away. The lines on the wood paneling behind him got clearer.

"Looks like we have some thinking to do," Merrie said. "I can't believe he's back."

"John or Mr. Nightmare?" Marcus asked. I think he meant it as a joke, but it didn't come off as one.

"Both. It's crazy," Merrie said.

"Yeah," I said. "It is, but let's get out of here. I don't want to be here any longer than we have to."

CHAPTER 15

We should have been a flutter of emotions after talking to John. The car should have been filled with excitement and eager voices brainstorming the best way to help him. It *should* have been that way, but it wasn't. The drive home was silent, contemplative. The air in the car was heavy, pregnant with a sense of dread that weighed on me as I sat in the front seat, watching the trees and houses pass by on our way back to Marcus's office.

No one spoke until Merrie put the car in park in the mostly empty parking lot. When we were kids, I was always trying to figure out who the leader of the Nightmare Club was. Sometimes I thought it was Chuck because he came up with the rules and was usually the most responsible. Other times, it was John —the whole thing was his idea to begin with. After Chuck died and John disappeared, it was probably me because I did everything I could to keep the Club going, even after all the loss we'd been through. When Mr. Nightmare was around, it was Merrie and the attitude that came from out of nowhere. It never seemed like Marcus was the leader until Merrie put the car in park. Marcus, who'd been the most resistant to the whole idea.

Marcus, who even earlier that day had worried more about his job and his future than helping his friend.

"We have to figure out a way to get more nightmares," Marcus said. "I don't have a clue what John needs the nightmares for if Mr. Nightmare is taking them from him. But if John thinks he can get out of this with more nightmares, then we should do what we can to help him."

Again, the car was silent. He was right, but I was at a loss.

"What are we going to do?" Merrie said. "We can't go out into the woods at night and tell stories. That won't work, right?"

"No," I said. "There's other stuff we can try though."

"Like what?" Marcus said.

"You guys won't want to hear it." My voice was quiet and low.

"Not for nothing, Anna," Merrie said. "But after this kind of day, I think we definitely want to hear it. What is it?"

"Well, I'm not really a drug person. I've only smoked weed. But I was friends with this guy at school who started to get big into different drugs. One of the ones he always talked about was LSD and mushrooms." I stopped and looked back at Marcus and then at Merrie to see their reactions. Their eyes weren't bugging out of their heads, but their silence told me enough of what I needed to know. They didn't say anything, so I continued on. "I don't really remember everything he told me because I'd been drinking and well, we slept together a few times. He liked to talk about it after we had sex and I was in and out of sleep usually. Anyway, he told me something like low doses of LSD make your REM sleep longer and that makes your dreaming more vivid…"

"Which would lead to more nightmares," Marcus finished the sentence for me. Once again, there was no noise in the car.

It was a huge leap to take. John needed our help, but would he want us to drop acid to save him? I didn't know. The John I knew when I was younger wouldn't. But he'd changed. And we didn't know how bad it was for him over there—the Nightmare Realm, he called it. Maybe he was in intense, unending pain. If that was the case, it would be worth it. I didn't know much about the long-term effects of using LSD or mushrooms, even in a low dose. My thoughts jumped from one question to the next, and the long silence in the car told me I wasn't the only one trying to figure things out in my head.

"Alright. Listen," Merrie said. "Even if we decide that is something we are going to actually do, we aren't going to do it tonight. So, let's think on it and do what we can right now. I don't think telling scary stories in the woods will cut it, like we said before. But we can rent horror movies or read horror books, right?"

"Right," Marcus said.

"And if it doesn't work?" I said. I didn't really want to say it. I wanted movies and books to be the answer, but I couldn't get my mind off the alternative. If we needed to help John and the usual stuff didn't, it was our only other option.

"Let's cross that bridge when we get to it," Marcus said. "It's not a problem for right now. Let's see what we can do on our own. I have to work tomorrow."

"Me too," Merrie said.

"Same," I agreed. Although, it wasn't until later in the day, I still had to get to work at some point.

"Okay," Marcus said. "Let's all go home, try a horror movie or book tonight. Or both. And we'll catch up tomorrow."

"Okay," I said. "I work until at least one in the morning, usually."

"No problem," Merrie said. She looked back at Marcus. "Marcus and I will be there for dinner around seven."

"Sounds good," I said.

Marcus opened the back door and got out. Merrie and I got out too. We firmed up plans and talked for a few more minutes in the parking lot. Merrie and I both hugged Marcus goodbye—

though Merrie also got a kiss. I got back in the car and gave them their privacy. I grinned at Merrie when she sat down behind the steering wheel.

"What?" she said. "I told you it was an on-and-off thing with us. It just happens to be an on thing right now." She backed the car up and turned out of the parking lot toward home.

"I know it's on again and it's none of my business, but do you think you two will end up together? Like just stay on again forever. Even when you're not together, you're still best friends."

"We probably will," Merrie said. "I don't know, it usually feels like a fling when we get back into this spot, but this time it feels different, you know?"

"How?" I said.

"It's hard to say. He's so serious and dedicated to his work, and I'm going to be an RN soon. Maybe because we're both doing adult things now instead of kid things. It feels like an adult relationship."

I shrugged. "It makes sense." I didn't know much about long-term relationships and we both knew it. I had a few boyfriends in college, but nothing serious, and I was never really on the look-out for a guy to be with. Deep down, I think I was still waiting and hoping John would find a way back and we could try out the relationship that never even got started.

I thought Merrie was taking me back to my house, but she slowed and turned into another parking lot.

"What's up?" I said, looking at her and not at where she had pulled into.

"Let's pick something out." Merrie pointed through the windshield at the sign in front of us. It read: *SuperStar Video*.

I laughed. "Sure, let's see if we can find something new. Are we watching together or are we each getting a movie to watch on our own?"

"You sleep late, right?" Merrie said. "Let's order Domino's

and watch a movie or two at my place. This night doesn't have to be all bad."

"Sounds like a plan," I said. We went in the video store to find a couple horror movies.

CHAPTER 16

After watching the movies at Merrie's house and then walking home, I *did* have a nightmare that night, but it had nothing to do with what I saw on TV. The movies—for the most part—were unmemorable. What stood out most from the previous night was the way everything seemed to be taking a step backwards. It wasn't 1995 anymore, it felt more like 1985. Merrie and I sat on her couch watching movies like we used to, as if nothing had changed but our ages. We were as close as ever because of another secret we shared, and Mr. Nightmare was still out there trying to hurt our friend.

My nightmare was about him—about Mr. Nightmare. His presence was unforgettable, and there were times when I could close my eyes and see him. Lying in bed, tired with a combination of anxiety and mental exhaustion, I thought I could see him. If I looked hard enough, he was there, in the corner of my room, part of the shadows but also a real part of my world. His top hat was down low so the weak moonlight couldn't reach his face, and he came toward me. I woke up and flicked on the light by my bed. Of course, he wasn't there, but I decided to sleep with the light on for the rest of the night—just in case.

I fell back asleep and dreamed again. Mr. Nightmare was

there, but we weren't in my bedroom, we were in Chuck's room. Chuck was sleeping on his bed and I was in the doorway trying to wake him up. Mr. Nightmare stood vigil at the foot of his bed watching him, waiting for him to wake up and look at him so he could kill my brother once again. I screamed and tried to run toward Chuck but my voice was gone and my legs were stuck to the floor. In the dream there was nothing I could do. Mr. Nightmare was going to kill my brother again and I was doomed to stand and watch it all happen. A bystander and witness to the murder of my brother.

Eventually, Chuck did wake up in my dream. Instead of sitting up and looking at Mr. Nightmare, he turned to look at me. His eyes were black marbles and his mouth twice as wide as it should have been. He opened his mouth and screamed at me. I covered my ears and Mr. Nightmare turned to look at me too and tipped his hat back. It wasn't the strange, inexplicable face I'd seen before; it was John's face. But, like Chuck, John's eyes were obsidian and his mouth was too big.

"John." I moved my mouth to say his name but no sound came out. He opened his mouth wide, his jaw unhinging like a snake about to swallow a large rat. Then John came at me, his mouth enveloping me. I screamed and woke up in my bed, my blankets a twist of damp, sweat covered fabric between my legs and around my body. I sat up, my heart pounding, my breathing hard and fast.

"There you go, John," I said, thinking about the nightmare. I hoped I was able to help him out a little bit, even if it wasn't enough to make a difference. Maybe it was; I didn't have a clue.

The brown digital alarm clock next to my bed read 6:45. It was early enough that I wished I was still sleeping, but late enough for me to recognize the fact that I wasn't going to fall back to sleep. The sun was most of the way up and the morning birds were signing outside my bedroom window. If Dad hadn't left for work yet, it was close to the time he usually did, so I climbed out of bed, went to the bathroom, then shambled my way into the kitchen.

Dad was just walking out of his bedroom and was pulling the door closed silently behind him.

"Hey," I whispered when he came into the kitchen dressed in his work clothes.

"Mom's still sleeping," he said and put a finger to his lips. "You up early?"

"Yeah, couldn't sleep," I whispered.

Dad made a coffee and grabbed two granola bars from the cabinet. He stuffed the bars in his pocket and poured the hot coffee into the Styrofoam cup he'd kept and rinsed out from his favorite coffee shop.

"Alright. You working tonight?" he said, obviously running late for work.

"Yep, I'll be in late again," I said.

"'Kay, love you." He came back and kissed my cheek on his way to the front door.

Once he was gone, I grabbed a banana and went out onto the back porch. The air was warm and humid and I could tell it was going to be a hot summer day. One of those days you didn't want to be outside when the sun was up. I felt tired, but knew I'd feel better after a run, so I finished the banana and did some light stretching before heading inside to get dressed and grab my Walkman. After a big glass of water, I took off, hitting the road before the sun was too high in the sky. I made it about halfway through my five-mile loop when the music in my ear began to slow and warble, a tell-tale sign the batteries were about to die.

"Shit," I said. The only thing worse than having my Walkman die in the middle of a run was forgetting my Walkman completely. If I didn't have music to listen to, I got bored easily.

I was two-and-a-half miles from home either way, so I kept going. I'd heard before that running without music made you better because you could hear your breathing and the pace of your footsteps on the pavement. While I understood the concept, I could never see myself running without music blaring in my ears. But since I didn't have much choice at this point, I went with it. I pulled the headphones off my ears and let them hang around my neck while still holding on to the tape player. I fell into a good rhythm. I listened to my breathing and tried to hold it steady as I ran up and then down a medium-sized hill. I listened to my footfalls too. I tried to keep them in rhythm, as if I was listening to one long song while my feet on the pavement kept the beat. It was hypnotizing. I kept my eyes up, watching my surroundings like I always did, but instead of music as a soundtrack, I created the sounds myself.

I went on that way for about six minutes. There was a short street with no houses on it that connected a nearby neighborhood with Prairie View. Along one side of the street there was a small section of woods, with an open field on the other. The houses were in sight, but there weren't any along that stretch of road. Because I didn't have my headphones on, I could hear more of what was going on around me, and when the wind picked up considerably, I noticed. The air blew against my ears and the side of my face, and the leaves rustled on the trees; branches bent and swayed in the wind.

My first thought was there was some storm moving in. They didn't usually happen in the early morning—thunderstorms typically arrived in the late afternoon or evening—but it wasn't unheard of to be awoken by a clap of thunder. Still, I looked up to check anyway. The sky was clear. The trees right next to the road swayed faster, moving back and forth almost in rhythm with my feet hitting the pavement. The other trees—the ones not right next to me—were not moving back and forth. The tops of every tree, in fact—except for those right next to me—were still. This wasn't a weather phenomenon. My heart skipped a beat and my stomach dropped. This was something else. And it wasn't from this world.

I slowed, thinking it was John trying to get in touch with me again. My breathing was already fast, but even when I stopped running, I couldn't catch my breath. I put my hands on my hips and stood looking into the woods. The sun was bright, but the woods were still dark. I peered through the trees, at first seeing nothing, and then a shadow moved out from behind one of the trees. It was tall and thin and stood almost like another tree, mixed in among the rest. It wasn't another tree though. The tall shadow moved toward me, getting closer, seemingly growing taller. It was still over a hundred feet away; I had time to run. I didn't. Not yet. I had to know for sure if it was really him, then I would run.

I took a half step back as the shadow became a figure. It wasn't gliding through the woods anymore either, it was walking. And it wasn't just any figure. I saw the top hat and the long thin arms and knew it was him. It was Mr. Nightmare.

As I turned to run, taking another step away from the man who killed my brother, his voice echoed around me.

"It's been a long time, Anna-banana," he said in the deep, mocking tone that made my skin crawl with revulsion and anger. I'd dreamed about his voice for years, thought about it in the dead of night more times than I could count. But I'd always been comforted by the fact that we'd killed him—I was scared only of his memory. That comfort was gone. John had said Mr. Nightmare was still alive, but until now I hadn't seen it for myself. Then, the sun hit the top of his hat and he held the brim of it, looking as if he was about to lift his head up and let me see his face. I realized then that it was real, what John told us had been real. Mr. Nightmare was back.

Whatever spell held me in place when he was coming toward me broke when he started to lift his hat. My stomach lurched at the thought of having to see his face again. I turned and ran. Not the easy measured pace of someone out for a long five-mile run. No. This was the dead-on sprint of someone running away from their worst fear. I might have

73

screamed too, but I can't be certain. All around me his laugher echoed.

I sprinted to the end of the street without looking back. I had to turn right at the end of the road to get home, and when I did, I looked back at the same moment he stepped back into the woods. The trees above him—and all around us—were still once again.

I didn't slow down, continuing my sprint through the neighborhood, up our driveway and into the house. Only when I got through the front door did I stop. My breathing was deep and heavy. The combination of the workout and the fear made it difficult to suck in the air I needed fast enough. I laid on the living room floor with my hands above my head and my feet splayed out to either side. My chest heaved as I forced my body to relax and slow itself down.

"Anna," Mom called from the back of the house—either from her bedroom or the bathroom. "You okay?"

"Yeah, Mom," I lied between breaths. "Just an extra-long run today, and it's hot out."

Chapter 17

Once I calmed down and caught my breath, my first thought was to call Merrie or Marcus. They were both at work though, and while there was now an impending danger, Mr. Nightmare had never done anything to us in public or with other people around. There was no reason for me to believe he was going to hurt them while they were at work. I figured if I stayed home and I knew the other two members of the Club would be surrounded by people all day, I could be relatively certain they would be okay.

I decided it was best to stay around other people too, so when Mom said she was going grocery shopping later, I told her I'd go with her. When we got home, I rested in bed—with my door open—for a little while and then started to get ready for work.

Jenn would be at work and she'd ask about how things went after I called out the day before. I could lie to her up to a certain point, but she was smart and would put two and two together when Merrie and Marcus showed up at the restaurant. Jenn was a close friend now, and I hated lying to her. It might get to the point where I had to let her in on the secrets of the Nightmare

Club. I added that to the list of things I had to talk to Merrie and Marcus about.

It didn't take long after I walked into work for Jenn to bring up the night before.

"Hey," she said from behind the bar, already prepping her side. "Everything go okay yesterday?"

"Yeah," I said, trying to sound nonchalant. I went to my side and started prepping for service. It would be a slow night, but we still had to be ready. "Everything went good. They might come in for dinner though. They want to get a *good* mixed drink this time," I teased Jenn, knowing she'd give it right back. Which, of course, she did.

"So, when you see them, just be sure to send them over here, then." She turned around and started to go through the bottles we had lined up against the mirror, looking for ones that were low or might need to be replaced before the end of the night.

"Right." I sliced through a pile of limes.

It felt like a regular night and I hoped everything would go smoothly the rest of the time. It did for the most part. It was slow, as expected, and there was lots of joking around behind the bar. A few of the regulars came. I mostly pulled beer from the tap or opened bottles of beer and wine. Nothing out of the ordinary. It was good and I almost forgot my run-in with Mr. Nightmare earlier in the day. Almost.

Marcus and Merrie came in exactly at seven. Like they'd been in the parking lot waiting until the clock switched over to seven to come inside. I caught Merrie's eye and pointed to two empty seats at the bar. They came over, said a quick hello, and ordered their drinks. I knew Merrie wanted a beer but there was no way I was going to serve her one. I could get in trouble enough for telling them to sit at the bar, but I knew Jenn wouldn't mind as long as I wasn't giving Merrie alcohol. When I gave Marcus his beer, he looked at me and his face changed. His mouth dropped and he went from friendly to serious in a heartbeat. I looked behind me, expecting to see something there that caused his drastic change in mood, but there was nothing out of the ordinary.

"What's wrong?" I said. He looked at me first, then at Merrie. I thought I was hiding the fact that something had changed pretty well. Jenn didn't say anything and she knew me well enough to notice a change, but apparently, I wasn't hiding it from my oldest friends.

I raised my eyebrows and slid two menus across to them, then glanced over at Jenn who was talking to a customer at the other end of the bar. I knew she couldn't hear me.

"I had a visit from our friend," I said, slipping back into the code we had used for Mr. Nightmare as kids. Then I reached over and pointed at something on the menu like I was giving them suggestions in case Jenn looked over. The last thing I wanted was for her to overhear us.

Merrie looked down at the menu and spoke under her breath, "You talked to John again?"

"Nope," was all I had to say. Merrie's eyes got wide and Marcus swore under his breath.

"I thought John said…" Merrie started, but stopped when Jenn came over toward us.

"Hey guys," Jenn said. "Glad you got everything all settled last night."

"Uh, yeah," Merrie said. "Thanks for loaning her out to us for the night."

"Of course," Jenn said. "I can cover for a few minutes, Anna, if you guys want to chat or whatever. Just going to grab some food for Mr. What-time-do-you-get-off down there." She laughed and rolled her eyes, then walked down to the end of the bar and around the corner to the window for the kitchen.

"On my run," I said, as soon as she was out of sight. "He came out of the woods and talked to me. I didn't talk back; I ran the rest of the way home. I figured he wasn't going to do anything with people around. I didn't want to call you guys at work. Life is so different now, you know?"

They both nodded.

"I dreamed about him last night too," I continued.

"Us too," Merrie nodded.

"Maybe that's how he found us," Marcus said. "John was wrong though, we need to…" He stopped when Jenn came back around the corner with a plate of food.

"Jenn, I'll drop it off for you," I said, knowing she didn't like waiting on customers after they hit on her, especially middle-aged men with wedding rings on. It made both of us feel icky.

"I got it," she said. "Talk."

"No." I took the plate from her. "Take their order, they can't figure out what they want anyway, and I make bad suggestions. Maybe you'll be better at it than me." I walked down to the end of the bar and shoved the burger in front of the guy. He wasn't even making it look like he was watching the baseball game on the TV above my head. He was looking right past me at Jenn's ass while she talked to my friends. Typical gross man doing male things. I offered him ketchup for his fries and asked if he needed another drink. I didn't even try to be nice to him. Jenn's dad wouldn't care if the guy complained, and Jenn and I told him why. The hope with these kinds of guys was always to get them out of the place as fast as possible no matter how much money they wanted to spend. A big tip wasn't worth it for either of us. Luckily those type of guys were few and far between at Pete and Mary's.

When I turned around, Jenn was leaning on the bar talking to Merrie and Marcus, all three of them laughing. I walked back over smiling, looking first at Marcus and Merrie and then to Jenn.

"What's up?" I said when I got over to the small, huddled group.

"Just talking about you," Jenn said. "I was telling them your hatred for guys like our friend down there and how I can always sic you on them."

"Yeah," I said. "So, how's that funny?"

"I was telling her how that was always my job when we were together," Merrie said. She gave me a look. Marcus, Merrie and I knew she was talking about Mr. Nightmare but Jenn had no idea. It shouldn't have been funny but it was, and I started laughing too.

Marcus and Merrie put in their order, and they ate while I continued to work, going over to talk to them about mundane things for the rest of the night. They stayed until closing, obviously wanting to talk to me without anyone else around.

When the place was empty and Jenn and I were almost done cleaning up and counting out the tips, Jim went over to them. I stayed where I was but listened in to the conversation at the same time.

"I know you're friends with Anna. I just have to ask you guys to leave while we close up. She'll be out in a few minutes," Jim said.

"Oh sure," Merrie said. "No problem."

They got up, and Marcus even took his clean napkin and wiped down the area in front of where they were sitting. Then he and Merrie left while Jenn and I finished cleaning up.

"All set, girls?" Jim asked when he came over to us.

"Yep," I said. "Just finishing up now."

We counted the rest of the tips and split the money, then went out back like usual. I wanted to talk to Merrie and Marcus, but felt like I needed to be with Jenn for her after-work smoke, for moral support or something. She offered me one like always.

"Merrie and Marcus are cute together, huh?" Jenn said.

"Yeah, they've been on and off for a while. One of these times I hope it sticks. They are good together."

"I think they were hanging around to talk to you. You don't have to stand here with me." Jenn sucked on her cigarette and blew the smoke out her nose.

"You sure?" I said.

"Of course," she said. "There's obviously something going on. You can take care of it. I'll be here when everything is done."

79

"Thanks," I said. Then, for some reason, I kept talking. I don't know if I felt bad lying to Jenn or if I felt bad because she knew I was keeping something from her. "Sorry I can't give you all the details…it's just…"

"It's okay, Anna," she said. "You're one of my closest friends, but that doesn't mean we know everything about each other. When whatever it is, is over, if you want to tell me about it you can. If not, that's fine too. Either way you're still someone I'll be close with. It doesn't change anything."

"Alright," I said. I started to walk off and then stopped and turned back. "Thanks for saying that. I've been conflicted since yesterday."

"It's all good," Jenn laughed. "Go take care of that shit! See you tomorrow?"

"I'll be here," I said and walked around the side of the building to the front where only five cars remained in the parking lot, Marcus had parked his right next to mine. I went over to it and knocked on the passenger window. Merrie rolled the window down.

"Get in," she said.

My mouth started to move as soon as I got in the car and I didn't stop until the story was done. I told them about the nightmare I had first and then about when Mr. Nightmare came through the trees.

"Damn," Marcus said. "John seemed so sure Mr. Nightmare couldn't get at us. He said he didn't care about us anymore."

"What if he just wants John to *think* that?" Merrie said. "What if he made him believe it as a way to get him to relax or something? What if everything he's doing on the other side isn't to take over? What if he's doing it to get back at the punky kids who killed him?"

"Or," Marcus said, once again taking the leadership role and forcing us—mostly forcing me   to think about things we didn't want to have in our heads. "John's been over there for years, almost a decade. What if he's not telling us the truth?"

I opened my mouth to argue with him and then closed it. My first thought was to shut the idea down. Of course John wouldn't lie to us. We were his friends. But how much did we actually know about him after all those years away? We'd all changed as people. None of us were the same; what made us think John hadn't changed too—especially given everything he'd been though? There was nothing much to say after that. All three of us knew we needed to talk to John again. Only now we didn't know if he was still our friend or if he was just as dangerous as Mr. Nightmare.

CHAPTER 18

"This is fucking stupid," Marcus said as we pulled into the parking lot of his apartment complex, about fifteen minutes after deciding to go to the farm that night instead of waiting. We'd changed a lot since our early teenage years, but one aspect of our adult personalities matched: we were all impatient, and if there was a problem to address, we didn't wait around to talk about it later. As kids, we were content waiting until we *had* to discuss a topic, maybe hoping it would go away on its own. Over the years—and maybe because of our past experience with Mr. Nightmare—we must have learned that tackling a problem head-on is the best way to go about it. So, when the three of us decided to try to talk to John again, we didn't care it was after one in the morning. We knew we had to make a trip to Shaw's Farm. It made a little bit of sense; the middle of the night was the usual meeting time of the Nightmare Club.

"Probably is stupid," I said. "But there's a chance it's not the dumbest thing we've done."

"Plus," Merrie said. There was an edge in her voice that I liked hearing. She wasn't going to take any shit from John or Mr. Nightmare. "If John is fucking around with us, I'd rather know it than keep trying to think of ways to save his ass. We were talking about dropping acid yesterday for Christ's sake."

"Be right back." Marcus jumped out of the car and ran inside to get a few flashlights.

"We don't know John is lying to us yet," I said. Even as I said it, I only partly believed it. I hoped it was true, but I didn't know for sure.

"I hope you're right," Merrie said. "But I'm prepping for the opposite. You know how the other one liked to fuck with us and make us not really sure what to believe. Mr. Nightmare and John had a kind of weird relationship from the start, right?"

She was right. Best to be cautious. Marcus came back with the flashlights. He started the car and we headed to Shaw's Farm.

The road the farm was on was empty. Marcus flipped his headlights off when we got close to the farm entrance. It wouldn't make us invisible to anyone who happened to be watching, but we'd be harder to see. The entrance was lit only by the moonlight, so Marcus slowed down as we got close, then eased the car onto the dirt road.

"This place is even spookier in the middle of the night," I said. We couldn't even see the farmhouse or the silos up ahead, and pressed on solely because they were supposed to be there.

"Feels like it's taking forever to get there," Merrie said.

"I'm just going super slow," Marcus replied. "I think I can see the moonlight shining off one of the upstairs windows of the house." He pointed through the windshield. I squinted, and he was right. The house was up ahead. The rows of corn opened up on either side of us again. Marcus rolled the car onto the grass and down behind the house, in almost the same spot we'd parked last time. He turned the car off and handed out the flashlights. From my spot in the backseat, I moved to get out, but Marcus stopped me. "I think I should talk."

"What do you mean?" I said. I looked at Merrie but could

tell if this was taking her by surprise too. I was closest to John, it only made sense *I* do the talking.

"Listen, Anna," Marcus said. "Obviously, you and John had a different kind of relationship. You knew each other longer and there were…feelings there. I don't want those feelings and all of your memories of him to get in the way. We know what our *other* friend can do. We don't know what John is capable of. We need to plan ahead and be ready for anything. You know I won't let him fuck us over. And if he has no idea what we're talking about, then it's a different story. But I think, to start, I should talk. You're too close to him and Merrie is, well, Merrie can be a hothead."

I disagreed—about me, Merrie *was* a hothead—but it wasn't the time to argue. He was right about one thing; when we got upstairs in the farmhouse, anything could happen.

"All right," I said. "Let's go."

The old, falling-apart farmhouse had been spooky in the waning afternoon daylight; in the middle of the night it was terrifying. We held our flashlights but waited until we got inside to turn them on. The steps up to the porch were barely visible in the dark. I led the way, sliding my foot along the grass until I hit something solid and then taking a step up. I climbed the stairs with slow, deliberate movements and felt around for the front door. I found the doorknob and opened it.

"Let's turn these on now," Marcus said, once we were all inside with the door mostly closed behind us. We flipped our flashlights on, beams sending shadows up along the wall in strange shapes. I turned and let my light find the stairs to the second floor.

"Up we go?" I said, taking a step in that direction. Merrie nodded, Marcus did the same. The flashlights threw just enough light for me to see them clearly.

We went up the steps in silence; the creaks and groans of the old wood were louder in the quiet stillness of night. Outside crickets and cicadas sang and chirped, unknowing of the terror we were about to face. While the fresh open space outside paid witness to the symphony of nighttime sounds, the darkness inside was suffocating and claustrophobic. It was everywhere we looked and we could not get away from it. The only thing holding the dark at bay was the light of our flashlights, and the beams were so weak it felt as though the darkness could overtake them at any moment.

At the top of the stairs, we went down the hall and returned to the room where we'd first spoken to John. Last time, there were signs of his presence in the house. This time we heard nothing but our own breathing and footsteps and the sounds of night outside.

"John," I whispered, once we were in the room. Marcus shot me a look. "What? I'm not allowed the say anything?"

"John, hey buddy. You here?" Marcus said. Without planning it, we stood in the same place we'd been in the last time we were there. And we all looked to the space where John had appeared. This time he wasn't there.

We waited. When we were kids, Mr. Nightmare had appeared in John's room when we were looking for him. John had appeared in the farmhouse only a day before. The curtain between our worlds was thin there. If John knew we were there, he'd appear. It was an instinct. We played our lights back and forth across the wall opposite us and waited, none of us moving, none of us saying a word.

"I thought you'd come," John said from the darkness. His voice was strong, yet different than the last time. Many voices, all belonging to John, speaking at the same instant.

Our surprise was evident by the frantic movement of the lights around the room. I found him first. He was in the darkened corner of the room. His head down, baseball hat pulled down low, hair hanging around his face.

"Hey, John," I said.

"Anna-b," John said. "Sorry about that yesterday. I tried to stop him."

"You said he didn't care about us anymore," Marcus said. He took a step toward John. We all knew we couldn't touch John or even look at his face, but Marcus was angry; I could tell just watching his body language.

"I didn't think he did," John said. "He never mentioned it. He doesn't give me any more or less attention than anyone else. There are so many of us. He has us all trapped."

"What do we do, John?" Merrie said. I did my best to let them talk. Marcus wanted to take the lead, and for now I was okay with him doing the talking. I kept my mind working, trying to figure out what was real and what wasn't. John had become untrustworthy and—even though I couldn't see his face and his voice was different—I wanted to try to get a read on him to see if he was telling us the truth or bullshitting. They needed to keep him talking.

"Get me nightmares. If I can break out of where he is holding us, I can try to get rid of him again. I can save everyone. *You guys* can save everyone. But I can't do anything without nightmares. Anna-b, yours helped a lot last night."

"Thanks, I guess," I said. The fact that he could see my dreams surprised me, even though it was something I'd known about since he first disappeared. The fact he brought it up made it real and more embarrassing.

"There's nothing else we can…" Marcus said, but John interrupted him.

"Shit," John said quickly. "I have to go. More nightmares."

His body seemed to shimmer in place and then disappeared; our flashlights were pointed at nothing but the bare wall of the farmhouse bedroom. I turned to asked Merrie and Marcus if they believed him or not, but before I could get the words out, the door behind us slammed shut.

We jumped and turned at the sound, all of our lights turning to point at the door. My first fleeting thought was that the door shut on its own, the result of old unused hinges and a house leaning to one side as it fell into disrepair. The thought was only momentary because the same door squeaked as it slowly opened in front of us. There in the hallway stood the monster who had taken my brother's life. Still tall and thin, with a top hat upon his head, Mr. Nightmare loomed, various parts of his body illuminated by beams of light. I was frozen in a combination of fear and anger.

"Ah, the Nightmare Club is meeting here now," Mr. Nightmare's voice echoed all around us. It filled the entire house and seemed as though it echoed throughout the entire farm, interrupting the music being played by nature outside. "I preferred the other location to this place, actually."

He took a step toward us and ducked his head to enter the room. All three of us took a step back.

"What do you want?" Merrie spoke up, and actually took a step forward as she did so.

"Oh, the little bitch. How I have missed all three of you." Mr. Nightmare spread his arms out to the side. He looked the same as I remembered him—as if no time had passed at all. But something John said made me take a closer look at him. He was different somehow. He'd always been a cocky, arrogant prick, but there was something else in his mannerisms and his voice, and I couldn't quite put my finger on what it was.

"What do you want with us now?" Marcus said. "We got rid of you once, we can do it again if we have to. You don't scare us like you used to." Marcus tried to sound tough, but even as he said the words, I bet he regretted them. He didn't sound tough, more like a little kid trying to prove to himself he wasn't scared by saying it aloud. The reality was, he was terrified. All three of us were.

Mr. Nightmare must have sensed the same thing because he exploded with laughter, even throwing his head back. When he did, there was a brief moment when his face—the vile, indescribable thing sitting atop his impossibly thin neck—was almost visible. I did my best to look away. Luckily, I only saw part of it. For a brief moment a wave of dizziness passed over me, and then it was gone as his face returned to the darkness. I glanced around the room for an escape. There were two windows just above the roof of the porch. We could climb out the windows to the roof then maybe drop to the grass from there, but Mr. Nightmare would probably follow us. We were stuck in this room with him.

"Not only do I still scare you," Mr. Nightmare went on. "I believe I scare you more than before, boy."

Next to me, I could see Marcus's lips tighten. If it had been anyone else, Marcus would have been pounding the guy in the face. *This* guy didn't even have a face.

"Whatever," Merrie said. "You could kill us if you wanted to, but obviously you haven't. So why not? What do you want us for now? You need more dreams or something? You want to suck our dreams like you sucked on your mom's tit? Tell us, or leave us the fuck alone."

It sounded like Mr. Nightmare blew air out of his nonexistent nose as his head turned to look at Merrie.

"I decided to pay Anna-banana here a visit earlier, and I missed my favorite—though shrinking—group of story-tellers. There were five of you once, now there's only three, but you're still my favorite." It was my turn to hold back from going after the guy. "But my friend Jonathan brought you all together, and since you were here, I thought I'd come by and say hello. You don't mind, do you? Oh, he is right about one thing, please keep the nightmares coming. They are *very* helpful. Especially the one you had last night Anna-banana. I particularly liked that one."

He took a massive step forward and kept coming toward us as he spoke. We backed up as he approached but soon ran out of room, our backs hitting the wall behind us. We were taller than we'd been ten years before, but he still towered over us and seemed to surround us when he stretched his arms out to either side.

I couldn't speak. His hand went to his hat and I knew what

was coming next. I'd dreamed about this moment so many times. I'd thought about what I should have done as a kid. I was faced with it again and I was still frozen with fear, my reaction the same as it had been ten years earlier. I wanted to slam my eyes shut but was unable to look away. Mr. Nightmare pulled his hat off, and even in the low light, his face was visible. There was a scream. I don't know who it was because I heard it and then the world spun and I saw nothing.

CHAPTER 19

I was the first one to wake up. The room was dark except for the light from one flashlight shining against the wall next to me. My face was wet, as was my crotch; my head pounded. I pushed myself up on my elbows, at first not remembering Marcus and Merrie were in the room with me. When I straightened my leg, it hit something and I sat up, seeing a body there on the ground next to me. I didn't know who it was. All I could see was a dark lump in the low light.

"Merrie?" I called into the dark. "Marcus?"

Someone groaned. I turned and reached for the flashlight, then pointed it at the moving dark lump. Marcus looked back at me, squinting into the light.

"Fuck, that was terrible," he said. "Turn that shit off."

Merrie coughed and stirred next to him.

I shined the light on her until she called out to me, then flipped it off. I wiped my arm against my cheek. I didn't need a mirror to know my face was covered in vomit and my pants wet with urine. Mr. Nightmare was terrible on his own, but the aftermath of a confrontation with him was terrible in its own right. When I was a kid, I didn't know the feeling, but now I recognized it as the worst hangover I'd ever felt.

"You guys okay?" Merrie said.

"Don't know if I'm okay," I said. "I'm alive though."

"Fucking pissed myself," Marcus said.

"Me too," I said.

"I didn't, but I'm covered in puke," Merrie said. We got to our feet. My head still throbbed, but standing actually made it feel a little better. Marcus got to his feet, wobbled, and put two hands on the wall to steady himself. Merrie coughed again but seemed no worse for wear once she was upright.

"This sucks," Marcus said. "Just another reason to hate that guy. Let's get out of here."

We gathered the flashlights—the batteries had died in two of them, then we worked our way down through the house and outside. It was not as dark as I'd originally thought. There was a light blue tinge to the dark sky, just over the stalks of corn surrounding us. Morning was upon us. We staggered to the car, took a few moments there to gather ourselves again, then left the farm.

"I'm supposed to be at work in a few hours," Marcus said. The whole car smelled like a combination of piss and vomit. I felt bad for him.

"I have to work later today," Merrie said.

"I can't call in," Marcus said through tight lips. He was pissed off. We all were. "Your car's still at the restaurant, right, Anna?"

"Yeah," I said. My mouth was dry and my lips felt as though they were stuck together. "I'll take Merrie home. Get to work. We have so much shit to figure out."

"Sounds good, and yes," Marcus said. "You working tonight, Anna?"

"Yeah, I can't take time off either after the other day," I said.

"It's okay. We're going to be exhausted until this is settled, one way or the other," Merrie said.

Marcus turned into the parking lot and pulled up next to the Dying Buffalo. Merrie and I got out; we were all so gross Merrie didn't even lean over to give Marcus a kiss goodbye. I didn't blame her, none of us wanted to touch anyone right now. We'd all feel better after getting home to a nice shower.

"Do you think John is setting us up?" Merrie said as the two of us drove across town.

"I don't know what to think." I shrugged. "We doubted John before, and it ended up he was trying to protect us. I don't know if it's the same thing now, or different."

"We don't really know him anymore, Anna. None of us are the same and we still live here in this reality."

"I know," I said. "He's not the John we knew. Even if we want him to be."

She nodded but didn't say anything else. I turned into the neighborhood and parked in front of Merrie's house. We said goodbye and I rolled my loud car around the corner and down the street to my house, rumbling up the driveway just as the first rays of sun were pushing their way through the trees and shining down on the roof of the house.

I turned the car off and put my head against the steering wheel. The headache was mostly gone. With a shower and some water, I knew I'd be feeling better—although still tired. At least I had some time to rest before work; Marcus was headed to work without any down time. He'd be a zombie by five o'clock when his work day was done. And I had a feeling he and Merrie were going to be at Pete and Mary's bar again later. We weren't going to leave this problem alone until it was solved. We had obligations, but having this *thing* with John and Mr. Nightmare hanging over our heads wasn't going to work long-term. There needed to be some end-game to all of it. It couldn't be ignored. Like it or not, when we left Marcus's apartment that day we'd reformed the Nightmare Club, and walking away wasn't something the Nightmare Club did for its members. And, of course, we had unfinished business with Mr. Nightmare.

After getting in and out of the shower, while avoiding my

still sleeping parents, I collapsed down into bed and fell asleep instantly. It was a completely dreamless sleep. One of those sleeps where it felt like I only blinked but hours had passed. When I woke it was almost one in the afternoon. I rolled out of bed and felt more like myself than I had since seeing Mr. Nightmare on my run earlier the previous day. Even thinking about it in those terms was surreal. After everything that happened, it had really only been a few days since we first talked to John in the farmhouse. It felt like a lifetime.

I felt better and got to work early, still feeling bad about bailing the other night and then leaving Jenn in the middle of her smoke break the following night. When I got there Jenn asked me how everything was going. I gave her a non-answer and hoped to keep the talk about Merrie and Marcus and what was going on to a minimum. It was another slow night. The place was mostly empty. There were only a few tables with people sitting at them. The rest were at the bar talking or watching whatever sports were on above my head. Everything was status quo until Marcus rushed in through the door at around eight with a look of terror on his face.

Jenn saw him at the same moment I did. She gave me a look and nodded. She knew something was wrong and was letting me know she had everything under control so I could talk to Marcus. I stayed behind the bar but went over to the side away from all the customers, where the wait staff usually put orders in.

"What's wrong?" I said, keeping my voice low and even-keeled. I hoped if I stayed calm it would rub off a little on Marcus, who was clearly on the verge of losing it.

"Anna, everything is fucked right now." Marcus did not feed off my calmness, and a few of the customers looked over at him. Even Jenn glanced over and raised her eyebrows. It was getting harder to keep her in the dark—she kept seeing too much.

"What's wrong?" I said, still keeping my calm demeanor

and reminding myself I got to go home, shower, and take a nap for most of the morning, while Marcus barely had enough time to shower and change. He was sleep deprived and at a mental breaking point.

"I saw them today, Anna. *Both* of them," Marcus said, he leaned in close but didn't lower his voice. I put my hand on his back and leaned forward so our heads almost touched.

"We have to keep it down, Marcus, or we have to go outside and talk, and that would only lead to more questions. Okay?" I said. I didn't wait for him to answer me though; I kept going. "Who did you see? Our friend?"

"Yeah. *Both* our friends," he said, again. "John and our *other* friend. I went out at lunch for some fresh air and they were in the woods across the street. Both of them, just standing there looking in my direction. I thought it was my over-tiredness—like I was delirious or something. So, I went back in and finished out the day. When I left, they were still. Fucking. There. Standing there watching me, or some shit."

"Okay," I said. My mind raced because all I could see in my head was Mr. Nightmare at the edge of the woods as I ran on the empty part of the road. I didn't think this was in Marcus's head. It meant two things; both worried me. First, it meant Mr. Nightmare was doing things differently than he did the last time, and showing his face when other people could see him. Second, it meant John was either helping him willingly or was being forced to help him. Neither of those things were ideal for my friends and I.

Marcus was freaking out and I needed him calm.

"Listen," I said, "they're not here now and they didn't come after you, so it's all okay. They won't do anything if there are people around. They're just trying to scare us. Stay here. Have some dinner and a drink, and we will figure this out."

Marcus took a deep breath. I heard him shudder when he blew it out. He wasn't okay, but he was getting there.

"Okay," he said. His voice shook and trembled with each

word. "I have to work again tomorrow, Anna. I can't do another all-nighter, but I'll stay for now. I left a message on Merrie's answering machine to meet us here after work."

Marcus ordered a beer and a burger. When I was at the tap pulling his beer, Jenn came over.

"Hey." Jenn nudged me with her shoulder. "Everything okay?"

"I don't know," I sighed, then in a moment of weakness, I kept going. "I think we might need help, Jenn, but I'm not supposed to say anything."

I knew as soon as I opened my mouth, I had made a huge mistake. Jenn was a good friend. She'd do anything to help me. The concern was clear on her face. She wanted to help, and I knew what she was going to say before she said it. But she never got the chance.

"I'm always here for you…" Jenn was only able to get the first few words out.

I just happened to look out toward the front of the restaurant at the right time. The large, front window of the place was only about three feet from the parking lot. It was normal to look out that window and see the front grille of a car. But when I looked up, I could tell something was wrong. The car was white and it was coming toward us too fast to be pulling into the first parking spot. It was racing toward the front window. I didn't have time to speak because by the time I realized it was happening, the front end of the car was up in the air and it was crashing through the front wall.

CHAPTER 20

Glass flew into the restaurant. The sound of it landing on the floor and hitting the tables was louder than the initial sound of the window shattering as the car tore through it. When I realized the car was coming in, I dropped to my knees, then grabbed Jenn around the waist and pulled her behind the bar with me. There were shouts from around us. Still kneeling behind the bar, I looked down toward the end. Marcus came crawling around behind the bar with us and we only needed to make eye contact for a second to know we were thinking the same thing. Mr. Nightmare had killed Chuck with a car and there was a pretty good chance he'd just driven one into the restaurant to take out Marcus and me.

"Everyone okay?" I heard Jim shout into the now mostly silent dining room. With the sound of his voice, I felt safer. Like I was a kid again, looking to an adult to provide safety—even though I knew no one was safe from the person most likely behind the wheel. I stood up and looked toward the window first. The car was halfway into the place. There was a small wall under the window, and the bottom of the car had become stuck on it. The front wheels were a couple feet off the ground, the back tires sat on the sidewalk outside. The car was motionless.

"Where's the driver?" someone said, as everyone inside stared at the car. I stared along with them. There was movement in car, though with the way the light hit it I couldn't get a good look. I was looking for a top hat and a driver hiding their face. Then I realized it wasn't just any white car. I knew that car.

"Oh shit," Marcus said under his breath. He had recognized the car at the same moment. It was too late for us to do anything. The passenger-side door burst open first. A dark figure climbed out with relative ease considering they had just been in a car that drove into a building. They slammed the door behind them. The person wore a baseball hat and had long hair covering their face. It was the first time I'd seen John in that much light. He'd become taller and skinnier—a lot more like Mr. Nightmare, now that I could see him clearly. He landed on two feet just inside the restaurant. He looked toward me—toward us—his head tilted to one side a fraction of an inch, as if acknowledging his friends. Then he turned and ran out of sight.

No one else in the place seemed to notice him. Marcus and I shared a look and waited for someone else to call out to John as he fled the scene of the crash.

A loud, metallic clang from the driver's side door drew my attention back. The door opened slowly, more like one should after a car accident. I saw the brown hair tied up into a tight ponytail in the small space between the car and the door, and I ran out from behind the bar to help the driver.

"Merrie!" I shouted as I ran past Marcus, Jim, and the other patrons of the restaurant.

"Hey, careful," Jim shouted. "Call 9-1-1."

I jumped over an overturned table and stepped up on a chair to get to where Merrie was. She looked wobbly, and her eyes couldn't focus on me.

"Merrie," I said as I stepped over another chair to get my hands around her.

"Anna?" she said, her voice distant as if she was not really there. I managed to get my arms under her armpits and pulled her out. Marcus came in behind me and helped me move her away from the car. She laid down on the floor.

"She was probably drinking," someone said.

I shook my head and said the only thing I could think of in the moment, "She's had seizures before, and she was supposed to meet us here. She needs help."

There was a flurry of activity, including the ambulance coming and taking Merrie, who was starting to come out of it. I relayed the cover story to a groggy Merrie right before the paramedics got there and hoped she was lucid enough to remember it when she got to the hospital later. If she did, the only thing she had to remember to tell them was that she'd had a seizure a week ago and this was a second one. They would put her on anti-seizure medication, but once she left the hospital, she could stop taking it. Luckily, she had been coming from work and there was no way she'd been drinking. I knew alcohol would be everyone's first assumption. The police took a statement from me and everyone else, but they talked to me the most because I was friends with Merrie. I kept the story consistent with what I told Merrie to say, and hoped she'd be able to remember enough to corroborate it. Marcus and I stayed with Merrie while they got her ready for transport. I listened to what she had to say, but kept an ear out for what the other witnesses were saying to the police. No one, not a single person, mentioned seeing a guy get out of the car before Merrie and run around the side of the building. Had Marcus and I been the only ones to see John?

Marcus wanted to ride in the ambulance with Merrie, but the paramedics told him he would have to follow in his car, so he did. I called my parents and explained the situation so they wouldn't worry. I told them I was helping clean up and then was going to check on Merrie at the hospital. There wasn't much to clean at the restaurant—most of the mess we weren't allowed to touch because it was a crime scene—while Jim got on the phone with his insurance company. Jenn kept giving me looks like she wanted to talk. I tried my best to look worried and upset so she wouldn't ask, but it didn't work. When Jim got off the phone, he came to me first and told me I should leave and go be with my friends. I agreed and headed out to my car without saying anything to Jenn. When I got outside—I had used the back door to get out—Jenn came up behind me.

"Leaving?" she said as she put her arm around me.

"Yeah," I said, slowing my pace but not stopping like I would have if I really wanted to talk to her. "Your dad said I could take off."

"Crazy night, huh?" Jenn said. She was waiting for me to say something more. I wasn't going to, though. I didn't want her to get involved. Of course, Jenn was the kind of person who would ask and not beat around the bush. "What's up with you guys, Anna? For real."

"What do you mean?" I knew exactly what she meant.

"Anna, I'm your friend no matter what," Jenn said. We turned the corner and came out around the front of the restaurant. There were still a couple cops there milling around as well as some people standing and checking out the car as it got picked up by the tow truck. We stepped away from the people. "There was obviously something going on before tonight. You told me you needed help exactly one second before your friend drove a car through my dad's restaurant. Marcus looked freaked the fuck out before that. I like them, Anna, but *you're* my friend, and I want to help you. Tell me what's going on, or what you need. Please."

I sighed. The last thing I wanted was to get Jenn involved with Mr. Nightmare. Too much could—and already had—gone wrong. But I was running out of things to say and do. I didn't want to block her out. I wanted to be a good friend. Was I being a good friend by keeping her in the dark and keeping her safe? Or was it better to be honest and tell her?

I could argue with her and hope it was enough to get her to back off, or I could use the approach I decided to take instead. I stopped when we were far enough away from the cops and bystanders at the front of the restaurant and turned to her.

"I know you want to help, Jenn. I want to tell you about everything. I—we—really need someone else to talk to. But I can't make the decision on my own. Okay? Let me talk to them and I'll call you. Will you be here?" I said, knowing I now had to have a difficult conversation with Marcus and Merrie at the hospital.

"I'll be here until Dad leaves," Jenn said. "Who knows when that will be. Call me here or at home. I don't care what time it is."

"Okay, I will," I said. "Thanks for trusting me."

"Of course," she said.

I turned and walked the rest of the way to my car and Jenn walked back to the restaurant. When I climbed in, I half expected to see John sitting in the back seat. He wasn't there though. If he was, I would have tried whatever I could do to kill him.

The Dying Buffalo turned on and I left the parking lot, headed for the hospital on the other side of town.

CHAPTER 21

When I got to the hospital, I found Merrie and Marcus in the ER. There was a police officer standing outside her room. The door was open, but the curtain was closed. Initially, the officer wasn't going to let me in to see Merrie. When I explained I worked at the restaurant, he reluctantly stepped aside. Marcus was sitting in a chair next to the bed holding Merrie's hand. Merrie had her head against the pillow and looked half out of it. Her eyes were partially closed, and even though she looked in my direction when I came into the room, I could tell she had no idea who I was. There were no other chairs in the room so I went and stood next to Marcus.

"How are you doing?" I looked at Merrie when I spoke, but didn't know what I expected for an answer.

"She's in and out of it," Marcus said. "They gave her some seizure medication. The side effects makes you drowsy, but it's worse at first because your body isn't used to it."

"Shit," I said under my breath.

"Yeah," he said. "And they do blood work to check that she has the right levels to stop seizures."

"Fuck," I said. "This is my fault."

"No," Merrie's strained voice said from the bed. She shook

her head slow but I could tell she wanted it to be urgent and emphatic. She opened her mouth to say more and her eyes drooped for a second. She tried again to speak but wasn't able to. Merrie looked at Marcus and waved her hand.

"Before the meds came," he said, his voice barely above a whisper in case the police officer was listening in, "she told me you were going to blame yourself if they made her take the medication. But it was the only way to keep her out of jail, most likely. It was a good idea. We'll figure this out."

Merrie nodded.

"Good news," a nurse said as she pushed open the curtain and breezed into the room. "Oh, another friend. Well, we got ahold of your parents and they're on their way. They should be here soon. When they arrive, we will ask that you two leave the ER room. Okay? You can stay here, and if she gets moved to a regular room you can see her there, but the limit is two visitors in these small ER rooms. Okay? Thanks for helping her though. It really makes a difference when friends or family are here."

There was some small talk as the nurse took Merrie's vitals and checked her IV drip to make sure everything was working as it was supposed to. When she was done, she left and pulled the curtain closed behind her.

"Did you find out what happened?" I whispered to Marcus once the nurse left. Merrie looked as though she'd fallen asleep.

"She got in the car after work and headed to the restaurant to meet us," he said. "The car was empty when she got in. She stopped at a light, and John was there sitting next to her. He didn't say anything at first, and then he reached over to her, his hand inches from her face, and she couldn't keep her eyes open. Everything went totally blank until she woke up with the car halfway inside your restaurant."

"I can't believe John did that to her" I said. I knew what Marcus's response was going to be.

"We should have never trusted him," he said. "It's not your fault, you know. He wasn't just trying to fool you. It was all of us. I don't know why, but now we have him *and* the other one to worry about."

"Yeah, I know," I said. "Thanks, Marcus. I feel like this is all my fault though."

"Nah." He put his arm around me. "We're in this together. We all trusted him."

We sat there until Merrie's parents came. They were happy we were there. We told them the story from the beginning—the one we were telling everyone else—even the part about her having a seizure when only Marcus and I were around the other day. Merrie didn't want anyone to know, we told them, and since she was almost a full-on nurse, we figured she knew what she was talking about. Her parents were disappointed in us for not letting someone know, but were thankful we were there for her. Still, no one else had said they saw John getting out of the car, and we didn't offer up that information. Shortly after we finished telling our tale, the nurse came back to Merrie's room and asked Marcus and I to leave. Her parents told us to go home, that Merrie was all right and they would take her home to rest as soon as she was released. As we left, we overheard the nurse telling Merrie's parents that blood tests showed no signs of drugs or alcohol in her system, which meant she could be discharged at any time. After hearing that, we didn't feel bad leaving. There was still one more thing I needed to talk to Marcus about. And there was, of course, the threat hanging over our heads. A threat, not just from Mr. Nightmare, but from John as well. And the threat had become more violent.

We made the slow stroll across the dark hospital parking lot. It was quiet, and though the emergency room was busy, once we stepped outside the doors, the beehive of activity melted away. The still of night should have been comforting compared to the assault on my senses in the ER, but it wasn't. The night held its own secrets. There was no telling when Mr. Nightmare or John would pop up next. The crickets chirped around us as we approached Marcus's car. Headlights flashed on Marcus first and then on me when someone turned down our row and drove past us on the way to the exit.

"You going to be okay?" He put his arm around me. Merrie wasn't gone, but right now it was just the two of us.

"Not till this is over," I said. I took a long breath and then spoke, knowing I had to say it before it became a big deal in my head. "Listen, Marcus, Jenn knows something is up."

"Yeah?" He didn't sound surprised.

"I called off work," I said. "Then you guys came the next night and I left before I usually do. Tonight, you looked like someone tried to kill you right before you walked in. Then Merrie…"

"I know," he said. "It looks pretty bad."

"She's a good friend," I said. "And she's not dumb. She cares about me and knows something is going on. I think I'm going to tell her the truth."

The statement hung in the air for a long time. Longer than I thought it would. I expected Marcus to shoot down the idea right away, but he didn't. He sucked in a slow breath and leaned with his back against his car, looking up into the cloudless night sky, as if the stars above contained an answer, not only to the question I was asking, but to all of our problems. The stars looked beautiful, but there were no answers in them.

"Sometimes I wish we'd never told scary stories in the woods," he said, still looking up at the stars. "Things would have been a lot different if we just said no to that part of being friends. Then at the same time, the best times of my childhood were with you guys—either in the woods or down at the Field. And I wouldn't trade those times for anything."

"I know," I said. I leaned against the car next to him.

"The last couple days," Marcus said. "I've been thinking about what Chuck would have done, you know? If he was still here, what would he be doing?"

I let him keep talking. I hadn't been thinking about Chuck very much lately, even though I was with Merrie and Marcus more than I'd been in years. It was hard to think about him when things were hard. I hadn't been ignoring his memory on purpose, but it was easier to deal with stress without thinking about him too.

"Chuck was, like, the leader," Marcus continued. "He was the responsible one and the organized one most of the time. We probably would have still hung out and stuff over the summers, but I don't think we would have been as close without Chuck. It might have been John's plan to tell stories in the woods, but I'm certain it was Chuck that made us the Nightmare Club."

"Yeah," I said. There had already been too much emotion in the day and I couldn't handle anymore. I could talk about Chuck for hours, but it wouldn't solve our problem. We'd already mourned Chuck; there would be time to remember him again, but I couldn't do it then. There were already tears welling up in my eyes and if I let them out—after the day I'd had—I didn't know how long it would take to stop them. Instead, I pressed forward, trying to use the emotion to force a resolution from this difficult conversation. "You know who I think the leader of the Club is now?"

"You," Marcus said. It wasn't a question. He was giving his answer, but he was wrong.

"No," I said. "It's been you, Marcus. It was Chuck, then John, then Merrie, then me. Now it's your turn. You've been right all along and you know what's best for our group right now. Thinking about what Chuck would do, that makes sense right now." Then came the hard part. "But Chuck has been gone a long time. We can think about what he would want, but in the end the question isn't what would Chuck do. It's what would *you* do?"

"I don't really know about all this John stuff. It's all happening too fast. I don't know what to do about John. I know Chuck would want you to tell your friend everything. I think the same thing, actually."

I smiled at him. We stayed there a while longer looking up at the sky and being in each other's company without talking or needing to. The night was calmer. John and Mr. Nightmare were still out there somewhere, apparently with the intention of hurting the three of us, but they felt far away for those few minutes. We said our goodbyes, then we left to go home for the night.

CHAPTER 22

The next day, around noon, I got a call from Merrie. She was home and resting. After telling her boss what happened, Merrie was granted the rest of the week, and all the following week, to recover mentally and physically. Merrie needed it. All three of us did. I could have taken as much time off as I needed, but I wanted to keep going in even though the place wasn't open. I asked Merrie if she was up for some company. Both her parents had to work, and since she was feeling fine, she made them go. Her sister had a summer job and would be gone all day, so she would be by herself.

"Is it okay if I invite Jenn over to your place?" I said. Then I hit her with the rest of the news. "I'm going to tell her what's been going on. *Everything* that's been happening."

"What?" she said. She sounded surprised, but it didn't sound like she was against it.

"I already talked to Marcus about it. He thinks it's okay, but I wanted to check with you first. If you don't want me to, I won't."

"Anna," Merrie said. "This is getting out of hand quickly. I don't know if telling her will help, but it certainly can't hurt. We can do it together."

I called Jenn and told her to meet us at Merrie's house, then gave her directions. I was nervous. We'd never told anyone outside of our circle—the constantly shrinking circle—about any of the things we'd experienced. I had no idea what Jenn would think. If I'd still been in high school, I would have worried about what people were going to say about me behind my back. It didn't really get much better in college; bullying was real and the thought that even my closest friends talked about me when I wasn't around never really left. Even now as an 'adult' I still often thought people talked about me behind my back; it was an ongoing struggle, but something I was working on. I never got that vibe from Jenn, though. She never talked about anyone behind their back—unless it was the older married men hitting on us at the bar. They were fair game in my book.

When I left my house to walk over to Merrie's, the humidity slapped me in the face as soon as I opened the door. We had air conditioners in all the windows of our small ranch-style house, and kept them running most of the time. You never really knew how hot it was outside until someone opened the front door. It was like trying to breathe in a cloud out there. The sun was hot, and the air was heavy and still. I was in the best shape of my life and was still sweating by the time I made the short walk to Merrie's. Her house had central air conditioning and the cool air on my damp skin felt great.

Merrie and I killed time and flushed a few of her seizure meds down the toilet while we waited for Jenn. She was there in less than an hour, with coffees for all three of us.

"I figured everyone could use some iced coffee on a day like today," she said after getting out of her car. I took the tray and carried the coffees inside. Merrie held the door for us.

"How are you feeling?" Jenn asked. There was a slight edge in her voice.

"Fine," Merrie said. "Sorry about the restaurant."

"It's okay. Not your fault. Seizure, right?" Again, Jenn spoke with a bit of an edge. I hoped this would go smoothly, but I was starting to reconsider my assessment. Merrie had just driven a hole through Jenn's family's restaurant. The place made money, but barely enough to stay above water; something like this might ruin it.

"Let's sit," I said, not giving Merrie the opportunity to lie to Jenn in this meeting where we were supposed to be coming clean about everything. We went into the living room. I sat on one end of the couch and Jenn on the other; Merrie sat across from us in a big leather chair.

"All right," I said, hoping to take control of the conversation as quickly as I could, but Jenn got going before I had the chance.

"Listen," Jenn said. "Yesterday was the worst day I've had in along time, maybe ever. I know you had a seizure or something, Merrie, and I don't really blame you, there's nothing you could have done. But I'm wondering why I'm here with the girl who ran through the front of the restaurant. I love you, Anna, and you're my friend, but I don't really understand all this."

"I know, Jenn. I totally understand, and please trust me when I tell you that..."

Merrie interrupted me this time, "I feel horrible about it. If you just hear what we have to say..." Merrie trailed off and looked at me, her eyes full of hope.

"Okay, sorry." Jenn took a deep breath. "I did ask for this, didn't I? I wanted you to tell me what was going on. So, I'll shut up."

"Yes," I said. "Let me try to explain everything. It's kind of a long story, so settle in and hold your questions for then end." I paused for a moment, wondering to myself if I really wanted to go through with this. Once I started and went into the story there was no going back. Once Jenn knew, there were no more secrets inside the Nightmare Club. Someone else would know. Maybe we needed it. Maybe we needed to make the circle larger

—at least one person larger. But there was only one way to know. I took in a long, slow breath and let it out.

"We talked about the Nightmare Club the other day. But there is more to it than just telling scary stories," I said. "I can't tell you the exact moment the Nightmare Club changed, but when it got bad, things went south fast."

Once I started telling her the real story of the Nightmare Club, my nerves were gone. I told her everything about the Club, about Mr. Nightmare and Chuck. I told her about what really happened to John when we were younger. And I told her about the events of the past few days and how they were directly related to what happened with Merrie and the restaurant. While I was talking it was like time stood still. I didn't look at Jenn or at Merrie the entire time. My eyes were focused on the floor, on the pattern of Merrie's living room carpet. I fell into my old role as a member of the Nightmare Club, telling a story —a scary story. And like with Nightmare Club stories, I'm sure Jenn was wondering the whole time if the story I was telling was real or fictional, and there was a chance I'd give her a nightmare.

One point for me.

When the story ended the room was quiet. The house was quiet. The whole world was quiet. As if everything stopped and waited for me to finish the story. Finally, I looked up. Merrie had tears in her eyes and a small smile on her face. I realized I had tears in my eyes too. I didn't know if it was from talking about Chuck or the entirety of our dealings with Mr. Nightmare that caused them. Jenn's eyes were wide, wild, as if she didn't— or couldn't—believe what she'd heard.

"Are you for real?" Jenn said, finally.

I shrugged. "You wanted to know what was going on. That's all of it."

"This guy—this *thing*—killed your brother? Don't you think it's possible it's just a guy and your head turned him into a monster or something?" Jenn was beside herself. She was doing the same things and asking the same questions we had ten years ago. But we saw enough to know it wasn't just some creepy guy. She was forced to believe it based only on our word.

"I know how it sounds," Merrie said. "We asked all of these questions. We assumed John was just out for points for a long time. But he wasn't. Mr. Nightmare is real and he's dangerous and he's come back for us again, for some reason."

"This is crazy." Jenn stood up. I thought she was going to storm out the door and leave, but she didn't. She went to the large picture window in Merrie's living room and stared into the front yard.

"Yeah," I said. "It is. But it's also true. You asked and you're my friend, so I talked to Marcus and Merrie and we decided to tell you. We need help, Jenn. We don't have an answer to anything going on."

"You think I'll have answers?" Jenn said. "If this is true, you guys are the experts, not me."

"We need ideas," Merrie said. "The only way we could get rid of him last time was to take the nightmares from him. From *inside* him. All that did was send John over to the Nightmare Realm, or whatever that *other* place is, and make him into a nightmare-person. Now he's trying to kill us too."

The sun was low in the sky and it was shining in through the kitchen window, projecting a long, stretched rectangle onto the carpet. I looked down at it, trying to think of something else to say. Jenn was one of us now. She was a part of this whether she wanted to be or not.

"You're a member of the Nightmare Club now, Jenn," I said. "There's only a handful of people who know about all of this shit, and you're one of them. I know it's getting late—though the restaurant probably isn't opening tonight. Marcus will be calling soon and I have a feeling we are headed back to the farm tonight. We need to come up with a plan. You can come with us if you want, or you can stay behind. You'll be my friend either way, but we need to know."

"If you take the dreams out of them, you become one of them, right?" Jenn still didn't turn to face us; she spoke while staring out at the front yard and the street beyond.

Merrie smirked at me. It looked like Jenn was getting involved.

"Yeah, that's right," Merrie said.

"You stuck your hand in him and you could touch the dreams, but then you pulled your hand out and you didn't take any dreams with you," Jenn said, clarifying the story I'd told her.

"Yup," I said. "Why?"

"So, at any point did you try to go…like, all the way inside him and not take any dreams back with you?"

I didn't say anything but looked over at Merrie. Her face told me she was as confused as I was.

"No," I said. "The only person who went all the way in like that was John, and he took hundreds, maybe thousands of dreams while he was inside Mr. Nightmare." It still felt strange saying his name out loud.

"What if being inside him is like going to the Nightmare Realm." Jenn said. "What if the answers to *really* killing them aren't here on our side, but on the other side?"

There was no way to know if Jenn was on to something or taking a shot in the dark like we had done last time. But right now, there were no other solutions. I liked her idea, but I could tell Merrie was still skeptical. It was weird how quickly Jenn got on board with everything. But I wasn't going to complain. We needed help, and she was helping.

"We don't know *how* to get there," Merrie said. "We only know what John told us about being inside Mr. Nightmare, and it wasn't much."

"John said at the farm the curtain between worlds was

thinner though, remember?" I looked to Merrie. "Unless you think that was just bullshit too."

"Yeah, I don't know." Merrie said. "I think he really did need us there, because everything started once we went there. So that must be a place where their power is stronger, or maybe the curtain really is thinner there and its easier for them to come over to our side."

"Right," Jenn jumped in, her eyes bright with excitement. "So, what if it's not just easier for them to come here, what if it's also easier for us to go there? Like a passageway or a gateway between the worlds."

"You're saying we should try to go there?" I said, following her logic. "See if we can do something to them there that we can't do here."

"Yes," Jenn said. She looked at me and then at Merrie. "Listen, you dropped a hell of a lot on my plate here today. And yesterday was pretty stressful, too. Maybe you're just fucking nuts and I am too. But I don't really think so. You said no one else saw that guy run out of the car last night, but that's not entirely true. I saw him."

"What?" Merrie said. I was speechless.

"Yeah," Jenn carried on. "I saw him but it didn't register right away because there was a fucking car in the restaurant. Then, when no one else mentioned seeing him, I assumed it was just like, my head playing tricks on me or something. Like it was a guy from the restaurant and in the stress of the moment I thought he jumped out of your car. That's all I thought it was until you told me it was different. Now I don't know what it means, but it seems like your friend, John, wanted me to know he was there. I don't know. Either way, it means I believe you and trust you guys."

"You're more trusting than I would be," Merrie said.

"Maybe I'm nuts too," Jenn laughed and sat back down on the couch finally. "But you asked me here because you needed help. I'm willing to help you—Marcus, too—so that's my thoughts."

The three of us sat there for a minute, no one said anything.

"What do you think?" Merrie said after we'd had time to think it through.

I shrugged, "I don't know if it will work, but it's worth a shot." Then I turned to Jenn, "You going to come with us?"

CHAPTER 23

M arcus arrived about an hour later. We explained Jenn's idea to him, and while he worried about the risk, he also thought it was the only choice we had. This wasn't like when we were kids. Mr. Nightmare wasn't sitting around waiting for us to tell stories and feed him dreams. He was coming after us. Were they tormenting us or trying to kill us? We didn't know, but we weren't going to sit around and wait to find out what was going on.

The air was still sticky and humid when we got into Marcus's car. It was late afternoon and sunny, but there were clouds on the horizon off to the west. Marcus, Merrie and I rode in Marcus's car and followed Jenn to her house to drop off her car. No one was there so she didn't even go inside; she climbed into our car and Marcus drove us to the farm.

The clouds seemed to be popping up from nowhere, possible thunderstorms in the distance. As we drove across town, I hoped this was our last trip to the farm. The sky was dark by the time we got there, but sunset wasn't for a while. Dark grey-blue clouds hung over the farm and most of the surrounding area. The temperature had been rising the past few days, along with the humidity. Today had been the hottest and the most humid, perfect conditions for a thunderstorm.

The car rumbled along the dirt road and Marcus eased it into what had become our parking spot at the old farmhouse. We got out of the car and all four of us looked to the sky; the clouds were building and growing taller as we watched. Thunderheads. Strong winds cut across the field and blew in our faces. It wasn't raining yet, but we heard rumbles and saw a few flashes of lightning in the distance.

"It's gonna be a bad one, I think," Jenn said.

"This is a terrible idea," Marcus said. No one responded. We all knew it was a bad idea, but we also didn't want this to continue on the way they had been. In the end, our desire to finish this and come to some sort of resolution, outweighed the fact that staying and going through with our plan was a huge risk. We didn't have to talk about it to know it. Instead, we took our flashlights and went inside.

It wasn't completely dark out yet, and we were still able to see once we were in the entryway. There was a loud clap of thunder, and the farmhouse temporarily lit up from a burst of lightning. Rain started almost as soon as we stepped into the house, and it got hard fast. The sound of the rain pelting the roof sounded like the buzzing of millions of bees above our heads.

"Let's go up," I said, and I started up the stairs. Our footsteps creaked all the way up.

"This is crazy," Jenn said from the bottom of the stairs. She was the last one to go up.

When I got to the top, I stopped, leaving room for the others to join me in the hall.

"You don't have to do this, Jenn," I whispered. Another loud boom of thunder and two quick flashes of lightning.

"I'm here," Jenn said. It was all the discussion there was on the subject. I walked down the hall and opened the door to the bedroom where we'd seen John the last two times. If he was in there again, things weren't going to be friendly anymore, and there was a good chance he'd have Mr. Nightmare with him. Last time we'd discussed who would do the talking beforehand. There was no such discussion this time. We were mad and we were going in to try to end this thing. I thought of it like our final showdown with Mr. Nightmare at the Dwelling.

"John, what the fuck?" Merrie shouted into the empty room, even before she was all the way inside.

The rain pounded harder against the roof now, directly above our heads. It sounded as if it had changed over from rain to hail.

"Come on, John." Merrie stepped in front of the rest of us, looking from one corner of the room to the other, the rage clear on her face. "Where are you? You drive me into a fucking building and then run away, and you can't come and confront me about it? Fucking coward."

Two rumbles of thunder in quick succession and the room strobed from the lightning outside. It must have been close because it was loud and both came at the exact same time.

"We might as well go," Merrie said. "He has super powers and he can't even show his face to me. We won't see him today."

A gust of wind shook the walls, followed by more lightning and thunder. It sounded like the world was ending outside the house. While we recognized the storm outside, we weren't focused on it. Inside we were calm. Merrie took two steps toward the door, her feet pounding on the floor, and she sounded so mad I actually believed she was leaving, but the door slammed shut before she got there. In the shadows, hidden behind the door, was John. His head was down in the all-too-familiar pose. The brim of his baseball hat covered the top of his face; the rest was covered by hair hanging down around it.

Lightning flashed and lit up the room for a brief moment. John cast an ominous shadow on the wall. The hail pounded down harder on the roof. None of us looked away from our former friend, now in the room with us. Jenn grabbed at my arm and I reached out and found her hand, squeezed it to reassure her. I didn't know exactly how this would turn out either, and I was hoping right along with her that we knew what we were doing.

"You know he was *always* right." John's voice drowned out the sound of the storm inside the small room. "You really are a little bitch."

"Fuck you, John," Merrie said. There was no fear in her voice. Every syllable was biting as she spat the words at him.

Our friend—our *former* friend—laughed and threw his head back, though he was careful to put his hand on his head to keep his hat from falling off.

"I always liked you the least, Merrie," he said. "I didn't want you to die, because then we couldn't get the whole Club back together again, but I was kind of hoping you *would* have died in the car accident. Then I wouldn't have to listen to your voice for another minute."

"What do you want, John?" I said. He was trying to get Merrie riled up; I needed to refocus the conversation.

"Anna-banana." He sounded more like Mr. Nightmare with every word. "You should introduce me to your friend before we get down to business. Nightmare Club business, that is." Lightning flashed again, brightening the room once more before plunging it back into almost total darkness.

"You know me, John. And I know you," Jenn said. Her voice was soft and weak sounding, but it was also firm. "Jenn Thornton."

John laughed again and the sound from outside grew louder, wind or even heavier hail, or a train coming at us, I wasn't sure, but it was as loud as anything I'd ever heard in nature. The tornado sirens began to wail. I knew the sound because every Tuesday they tested the sirens. Every once in a while we had a storm that brought the potential for a tornado, but I'd never actually seen one.

The siren distracted all of us—even John. For a split second, the roaring sound of the wind outside and the siren blaring, made us all realize what was happening. We knew what we'd see on the other side of the window if we took a moment to look. I used the momentary distraction to my advantage. Instead of worrying about the oncoming vortex of wind and dirt barreling down upon us, I sprinted for John. It hadn't been the plan for me to jump inside him right away; we were going to see what he had to say to us first, maybe find out what we needed to do to get him—them—to stop. But the opportunity was there, and I took it. John wasn't too far away, only a few steps across the room, and I ran as hard and as fast as I could. He turned toward me but I was already there. He was too late. I held my breath, as if going underwater, and ran right into him.

I didn't need to hold my breath, but jumping inside of him did feel like jumping into a bucket of ice water. I recalled when my arm was inside of Mr. Nightmare all those years ago and how it felt cold and damp inside him. When my body was absorbed inside John, I felt the same damp, cold feeling, but this time it surrounded every inch of me. I looked around. Just like last time, there were dreams in every direction. With Mr. Nightmare I'd recognized most of the dreams because we'd supplied so many of them. But here, inside John, I didn't recognize any of them. I felt them brush up against me. I avoided touching them when I could and pushed them away when they got too close. There was an obvious stress, but I knew what to expect this time and I was able to calm myself down and actually experience what was around me. At first, I thought there was nothing but darkness, dreams floating in an infinite void. But that wasn't true at all. My feet—which never left my world last time —were not floating around inside John like I expected. Instead, they were standing on something solid. I was inside him, but also not inside him. Had I made it? Was I in the Nightmare Realm? It was dark, and I saw nothing but the dreams. I was inside *something*. I felt walls around me. There was more to this place than I could see.

"Hello?" I called out, expecting my voice to be lost to the darkness. Instead, it echoed, as if I had yelled into a large empty room or a quiet library.

I took a few steps forward. My feet shuffled against dirt or a wood floor covered in dirt. I put my arms out, now certain there were walls or rocks or trees in front of me. A few more tentative steps forward produced nothing new. There was still a sense that I was inside of something, but I couldn't see or feel what it was.

"Hello," I called out a second time. My voice echoed again.

I stopped moving. There was a noise behind me. A shuffling sound, heavy breathing. John? Mr. Nightmare?

"Who's there?" I said, my voice soft, cautious.

"Anna?" It was Jenn.

"What are you doing here?"

"Where are we?" Jenn said.

"I'm not sure," I said. "Inside John, I guess."

"But this feels like an actual place." She shuffled toward me, and I could see her looking around, pushing the dreams out of the way until we were right next to each other.

"What happened back there?" I asked.

"The roof blew off the place and I fell forward. John kind of lost his balance and I lunged at him to come here," Jenn said.

"Are Merrie and Marcus okay?"

"I don't know," she said. "I'd never seen a tornado before, but it was right there, coming right for us."

"Shit," I said. "Let's keep moving. If John doesn't know what's happening yet, he might figure it out soon."

We walked through the darkness, our footsteps still echoing and crunching on whatever was beneath us. The dreams, once swarming all around us, became less concentrated, then very sparse so we could only see them if we stopped, held our eyes still, and focused on them.

"Jenn, look." I pointed in front of us; there was a faint, red light. If we had been somewhere else, I would have called it the sky, because it was above us and off in the distance, but I didn't know what it was.

We continued forward, using the red light as a guide, walking toward it. The light didn't get brighter, but it did get larger. At first it was only a small point of light in the distance, but as we walked it grew, stretching out in front of us. Then everything around us changed. We hadn't moved, but the red light brightened enough for us to see our immediate vicinity.

"Holy shit," Jenn said.

I couldn't even speak. What had once been nothing but darkness behind us became a long dark hallway, with a wooden ceiling and walls. Large thick beams guided us out of the darkness and toward the red light. The floor, as I suspected, was nothing but hard packed dirt, though there were little sprigs of reddish-brown grass sticking up at the edges. In front of us was a flat, barren landscape. It was mostly dirt, though there were also spots of reddish-brown vegetation poking up at random spots. The sky above us was mostly dark, black like a starless night sky. But shining down on us—brighter than a moon, but not as bright as the sun—was a flat red disk illuminating the place enough for us to see the horrors we were about to witness.

"Where the hell are we?" Jenn said.

"This is it." A voice from behind us made us both jump. "The Nightmare Realm."

CHAPTER 24

We both jumped and turned at the same time when the voice called out from behind us.

"John," I whispered to Jenn, and we backed away from the gaping mouth of the hall. Then, louder, I spoke to my former best friend. "What do you want with us?"

"Anna-b," he said as he stepped out of the darkness, his face hidden in shadow. "I don't want anything new. You knew I needed nightmares, that's why you kept that sorry excuse for a Nightmare Club going all those years. To give me dreams to feed off of. Nightmares. But come on, Anna, you know once Chuck and I left, the Nightmare Club was never the same. All I want now is what you wanted to give me then: Your nightmares."

We backed away as he continued his slow, measured approach. He wasn't in a hurry to get to us; I guess he didn't need to be. We weren't in our world, we were in his—the Nightmare Realm—and he could do things the way he wanted. He knew his way around and knew we were terrified. But I knew something about him too. I knew he wasn't telling the whole truth. Maybe he did want our dreams, but there was more to it.

"Why did you lie to us?" I said, still retreating. "You're *still* lying to us. We were trying to figure out how to get you dreams. We were going to do what you asked us, John. Marcus saw you with our friend outside his work. You put Merrie to sleep and made her drive a car through a wall. We would have helped you. We would have done anything for you, John. *I* would have done anything for you, if you'd asked me."

"I lied because I had to. I *do* need dreams, Anna. I need them, not because Mr. Nightmare is making me take them, though. Because I'm becoming more powerful than he ever was. He's not a bad guy, you know. Together we are going to control this place." As he finished speaking, John waved his arm toward us, gesturing to the world—Realm—around us. "I…" He started to say something else but stopped himself.

I looked again at the barren landscape and noticed things I hadn't seen the first time, either because they weren't there or because when John waved his hand, things appeared like he was some sort of malevolent, grotesque magician. Off in the distance, almost at the horizon line where black sky met nearly-black ground, stood a figure, glowing red in the maroon moon-light. It was not human, or even human shaped. It had eight long legs growing out of a small body, not unlike a daddy-longlegs lurking in the corner of the kitchen or by the down-spout of the gutters. Even from a distance I could tell it was gigantic. Closer, within a few minutes walk of our current loca-tion, was a crowd of human-looking creatures—Nightmare-people. Their limbs were longer and they were taller than the average human, but they were at least humanoid. Jenn gasped next to me; her hand went to her mouth. At first, I didn't know what she saw, then I noticed. The group of figures all had their heads hung down low looking at the ground. In the center of them stood a figure, a little taller than all the rest.

There was a top hat on his head.

The Nightmare-people around Mr. Nightmare stopped moving. He stood still, as straight and tall as he could, and his head turned toward us. From across the barren field, I felt his gaze upon me. My stomach lurched, knowing what would happen if I saw his face. The only thought I had was that I wasn't going to be leaving the Nightmare Realm alive.

The others around him bowed their heads in reverence or fear, I couldn't be sure which. He came toward us, almost gliding as his long legs carried him in our direction. I took a step back, then another, Jenn backpedaling with me.

"Nope," John said from behind us. I'd known he was there, but in the moment I still thought of him as my friend, and not as someone who worked alongside the terrifying monster who'd killed my brother. We were too close to John and I took a step forward, finding myself trapped between the monster I thought I'd already defeated, and the one who I used to love.

"Tell us what you want, John," I said. "We'll go back and do whatever we can to help you if you leave us alone."

I could see Mr. Nightmare's legs moving now, one long step after the next over the empty, dirty terrain until he was almost upon us. He slowed as he approached and stretched his hands out to the side. He'd done this before when he had Merrie and I trapped with the barrel behind us at the Dwelling. This time though, it was John who had us pinned in place. Jenn's breathing was hard and fast, and I could hear it even over my own strained whimpers. This was her first time seeing Mr. Nightmare, and he was even more ominous there, in *his* place.

"I don't believe we've met," Mr. Nightmare said as he stepped closer to us. I couldn't see his face, but his head was turned toward Jenn. His voice didn't sound like it did in our world. Here, his voice sounded normal, without the usual echo.

"This is Jenn," I answered for her. "She only wanted to help me and doesn't want anything to do with you. Either of you." I glanced back over my shoulder at John.

"Well, that's good," Mr. Nightmare said. "Because the feeling is mutual. But now that you're here, Jennifer, perhaps you should stay a while."

He waved a hand in Jenn's direction. Jenn shot backward as

if tugged by a rope tied to her waist. She screamed and rocketed out into the wasteland around us. A large dead tree rose up from the ground. Jenn's speed slowed and then stopped as she reached the trunk of the tree standing at least twenty feet in the air, its many dead branches reaching out in all directions. She fell to the ground at its base. Mr. Nightmare waved his hand a second time and the tree began to fold down around itself. The branches came down around Jenn, encasing her in a cage made entirely of the dead tree. I could barely see her between the branches as she scrambled to her feet and tried to pull, push, and rip at the old wood around her, but she couldn't break any of the branches. Mr. Nightmare laughed as she continued to struggle.

"Why don't you let her leave? You have me," I said, looking first at Mr. Nightmare, then turning back to John. He had changed, but somewhere in there I knew was my friend. Maybe I could coax him out of it.

"Sorry, Anna-b, can't do that either," John said. He walked around in front of me so he was standing next to Mr. Nightmare. John was a lot shorter than him, but my friend still had the same long thin limbs that Mr. Nightmare had. They both stood the same way too, with their heads tucked to their chests so I couldn't see their faces.

"How much of what you told us is true, John?" I said. "You told us he had you—and others—held captive, that he was farming dreams or something." I looked out at the others in the field who were still standing in a semi-circle, heads down, in the familiar stance.

"Not much of it was true," John said. Even though I couldn't see his face, I could tell there was a smile on his lips as he spoke. "I just wanted you guys to come to the Realm. I didn't think it was going to be so easy to get you here. I was hoping for all three of you. I didn't know Merrie and Marcus would abandon you like that. And I didn't know you were going to start telling strangers all about how you sent me here and left me for dead."

"What do you mean, 'sent you here'?" I asked, confused. My mind drifted back to that day in the woods, running through the events as they unfolded when John sacrificed himself for us, because we wanted revenge for what Mr. Nightmare had done to Chuck.

"You orchestrated the whole thing!" The anger in John's voice was palpable. Did he actually believe this at the time, or had Mr. Nightmare poisoned his mind? "You knew I'd step up. I loved Chuck too, and you knew I'd do anything for him. You came up with some fucking crazy idea and you *knew* I would do your dirty work for you because of Chuck. You let me jump inside him and maybe even knew I'd be stuck here. You got Mr. Nightmare out of *your* life and got to move on while *I* had to stay here. I had plans for my life too, Anna. You stole them."

Mr. Nightmare stood stoic next to John, seemingly content with letting us argue this out while he watched on. I didn't know what to say to him. How I could convince him what he was saying was untrue? Would he believe it if I told him Mr. Nightmare had been poisoning his brain all these years? Probably not.

My mind raced and I felt the stares of both John and Mr. Nightmare on me. They both waited for me to give an answer— Mr. Nightmare amused to see the evil plan coming true, John seething because of perceived betrayal.

"John." I tried my best to stay calm. I had to get Jenn home, maybe remaining calm and being diplomatic would deescalate the situation. "I understand you feel betrayed. I didn't want this to happen to you. Or anyone else. We made the decision as a group. I would have given my life for Chuck and I was ready to die for him that day. Don't you remember?"

"Don't start that again, bitch!" John snapped. "You know exactly what you did then, and what you're doing now."

I jumped back. It felt like I'd been hit. His words hurt, not only because he was my friend, but because I think deep down when I was a kid, I loved him. Not in an adult way, but in a middle school crush way. He was my person and when he left, I'd always compared other guys to him and wondered what might have happened if things had been different. I didn't want to cry, but tears welled up in my eyes. I didn't blink. I didn't want him to have the satisfaction of watching them drip down my cheeks.

"That's not true at all," I said. I didn't know what else to say, so I put my head down—mimicking the pose of John and Mr. Nightmare—hoping I wouldn't lose control and burst into tears.

"Well," Mr. Nightmare interjected. "I hate to ruin this beautiful reunion but I'm really at a bit of a loss here. I wasn't expecting you to come here for a visit, Anna-banana, yet here you are, and you brought a friend with you. I'm actually not quite certain what we're going to do with the two of you just yet. I'd like to talk to Jonathan here and see if we can't come up with something fun for the two of you to pass the time."

Mr. Nightmare stepped closer; he towered above me. I kept my head down. I wasn't going to look at his face no matter how much he tried to get me to look up.

"Don't worry," he said, as if he could read my mind—it wouldn't surprise me if he could. "You don't have to look at me just yet."

He waved his hand and I was thrust backward, pulled by the same unseen force that had pulled Jenn. A sound erupted behind me and for a second, I thought I was being pushed back into my world and the awaiting tornado, but I wasn't. My back slammed against the trunk of a tree, which hadn't been there minutes before. The air rushed from my lungs and I crumpled to the ground in a heap. As I sucked at the air, the dead branches of the tree folded in around me. I managed to get onto my hands and knees. I peered through the enveloping branches and saw John and Mr. Nightmare about fifty feet from me, laughing. Jenn was to my left but I couldn't see her through the branches of her tree. We'd been isolated, caged in the Nightmare Realm.

CHAPTER 25

The barren world outside my tree cage got dark and silent after a few minutes. The red glow from above was still there, as was the whipping wind which flung specks of dirt and sand into the branches of the tree holding me. There was a grating sound whenever the wind blew, like a vacuum rolling over an especially dirty carpet. Hopelessness moved in as well, with complete disregard for my desire to remain optimistic. I didn't know what to expect when I dove inside John back at the farmhouse. I had only those faint memories of thrusting my hand—with my mom's sewing shears attached—inside Mr. Nightmare. Even if I'd been thinking of a place like this, another world, I don't think I could have imagined *this* place.

Not long after my imprisonment, Mr. Nightmare and John left. I didn't see or hear them walk away. One second they were there, standing near the entrance to the hallway we'd walked through to get here, the next second they were gone. I didn't know if they were somewhere else in the strange Nightmare Realm, or if they'd left this place for my own world.

Neither Jenn nor I said anything for a long time. I didn't know if Jenn was awake. Maybe she'd learned too much too fast, her brain had overloaded, and she'd passed out. Or maybe she was pissed at me for getting her even remotely involved in all of this—if she was, I wouldn't blame her. Or maybe, like me, she was trying to figure out a way back into our world, where things would make a little more sense.

Again, I pulled at the branches. I slammed my foot into a thinner one over and over hoping to snap it or crack it, weaken it in some way so I could begin my escape. It bent a few times, but it didn't break. When I was exhausted and couldn't kick anymore, I stood up and leaned against the same branch hoping my body weight would break it. It didn't. I sat back down.

"No luck." Jenn's voice was distant, but loud enough to hear. I jumped at first, not expecting to hear it. When I realized it was her, I smiled. At least I didn't have to go through this alone. If she hadn't followed me here, I would have been in a single makeshift prison with no one to talk to. It was a small consolation.

"Good to hear your voice," I said. "I can't even get the smallest one to crack."

"Same here," she said. "What are we going to do?"

"I don't know," I said. It was the most honest thing I could say. A younger version might have told her we'd come up with something or reassured her that it was going to be fine, but I didn't know if it was going to be okay or not. If they wanted us to die, then we would die. There wasn't much either of us could do about it. "I have to think and try to figure something out, I guess. Maybe I can still appeal to John. He might be our only hope."

"Doesn't seem like we have a lot of hope then," Jenn said. The words were desperate, but there was a joking manner in her tone of voice. Then she laughed.

"What is it?" I smiled, not really understanding why she was laughing.

"Anna, he hates your fucking guts." She was laughing even harder now. "If he's our only hope, we're pretty much fucked."

I might have been mad at her in a different situation, but she was right. John did hate my guts, that much was clear. The brainwashing job Mr. Nightmare had done on him was thorough and complete. If John was our only way out, we were hanging on a thin thread. I was glad I had her perspective because Jenn was right. I couldn't rely on John anymore, no matter how bad I wanted to remember him like he was; that kid was gone even if my mind kept pushing me to believe otherwise. I started to laugh too.

"You're right," I said, sitting on the dirt with my back against the tree trunk and my feet pulled up under me. "He's not much of a hope, is he?"

"No," she said, and we laughed some more.

It lasted a few more minutes, as if the absurdity of the situation made it easy to laugh at. But then we both calmed down and composed ourselves. It was funny, but the reality was, we found ourselves at the mercy of John, Mr. Nightmare, and whoever else they decided to bring along to torment us. The thought was terrifying.

When our laugher died out, either from exhaustion, fear, or a mix of both, we returned to our silence. My entire body ached. The stress of the last few days was proving to be too much for me to handle. The wind gusted through the tree branches, and the stinging sand and pebbles came with it. I leaned against the trunk. There was nothing I could do. There was nothing we could do to change our situation. It wasn't hopeless—not yet, anyway—but we needed to wait for something to change. I closed my eyes, not to sleep but to wait. I hoped we could make it out alive, but I didn't give us much of a shot. I tried to push everything I was experiencing out of my mind. I needed to focus on something else to get through this.

I don't know how long I sat there, but when I opened my eyes, my thoughts were confused, my vision blurry, like waking up from an unexpected nap. It took me a few moments to get my bearings. I stretched my legs. My feet and my ass were pins and needles. I was able to stand up straight inside my small cage. I grabbed onto a few of the branches, stuck my face between them, and looked out into the Realm. I could see Jenn's cage. There was no movement inside and I wondered if she had succumbed to exhaustion. I didn't want to yell if she was sleeping.

The only other thing I could see was the opening to the hallway we'd entered from. The hallway had led to our world, but would we be able to get back if John or Mr. Nightmare weren't there? It was as if John had been a doorway. I entered through him and it led me into this world. If that was true, it might also be true that I needed him—or any of the nightmare-people—to travel though, like a conduit. Without a destination I might walk down the hallway forever without finding a way to leave. I stretched my back and twisted side to side, listening to each vertebrae crackle as I did.

With some of the anxiety fading from when we first arrived —because Mr. Nightmare and John were nowhere to be seen—I was able to better assess the place we were in. At first glance, I thought it had been nothing but a barren, dirt-covered waste-land. While it was mostly desolate, it wasn't as barren as I first thought. In the distance there was a small grove of trees. All of them were dead and—much like my cage—the branches twisted and turned in directions impossible for any tree I'd ever seen to grow in. The ground wasn't as flat as I first thought, either. I realized we were half way up a small hill and that we were actually overlooking a rather large depression in the land. The grove of dead trees sat atop an equally small hill on the opposite side of the depression. The hallway was actually more of a tunnel. The wooden top and sides were visible at the mouth, but eventually the wood was buried underneath dirt and dead grass. Because of the way the land rose around us, I couldn't see what was behind my tree-cage. I wondered if there was a village or some other structure that John and Mr. Night-mare called home somewhere out there.

"Anna," Jenn called from her cage. I looked over and saw

her standing with her face pressed against the branches in the same way I was.

"Hey," I said. Before I could get another word out, a gust of wind blasted sand and dirt in through the branches. I clenched my eyes shut, but the small particles stung when they found their way in. Jenn yelped and I knew the dirt had gotten her too. When the wind died down, I returned my face to the spot in between the branches. When I looked out, we weren't alone. There were a least ten wolf-like creatures standing about ten yards away from us, looking back and forth from Jenn to me.

"Oh shit," Jenn said.

CHAPTER 26

Like everything else in the Nightmare Realm, the wolves didn't look like normal wolves. The nightmare-wolves were tall and thin, their legs and bodies longer than any dog or wolf I'd ever seen. As if everything in the Nightmare Realm was stretched a little bit more than in my world. They were almost as tall as me, reminding me of when I was younger and came face to face with a Great Dane. They were all black and didn't have any fur—or if they did, it was short and matted tight against their skin, because I could see every muscle and tendon on their lean bodies. While their bodies resembled Mr. Nightmare's and the other creatures from this place, their faces did not. They had long snouts—like their faces had been stretched along with their bodies—and dark, inset eyes that stared at me with a look of anger and distrust. Their mouths were not closed, and it looked like they wouldn't have been able to close them fully if they wanted to. Instead, their lips were pulled back in a constant grimace. They had a long row of sharp teeth on top and a similar row of sharp teeth on the bottom, save for two larger teeth set into their bottom jaw and stretching up almost to the snout of the hideous beasts.

While the appearance of the nightmare-wolves was different

from any canine animals we had in our world, the noises they made were all too familiar. The growling and snarling of these creatures was easily recognizable. They were mad and wanted nothing more than to get at Jenn and I. My branch cage protected me, but I still backed away from the animals. They stared at us, growling with their heads down low, haunches up and legs coiled, ready to move in or pounce. They knew we didn't belong there. I'd stopped trying to figure a way out of my cage, but if I was still determined to get out, their mere presence was enough to deter my escape.

"Anna." Jenn's voice was lower, almost as if she'd tried to yell and whisper at the same time. I understood her apprehension. "What do we do?"

"I don't know," I replied in the same loud whisper. I didn't want to give those animals any reason to get closer. "But we're safe in here for now." I patted the dead branches, thankful for the wooden bars.

The nightmare-wolves could hear us, and it was almost as if they understood us because it was clear they didn't like what we had said. They came closer. Their heads were still low; they growled and drooled as they approached. Two of them loped over to Jenn's cage, the rest came toward mine. I put my back to the tree trunk, thinking it was as far as I could get from the nightmare-wolves, but there were small openings on either side of the trunk between the branches that came down around me. When the wolves encircled my tree-cage completely, I realized their long thin snouts might be able to fit through those small spaces. I moved to the center of the cage, hoping I'd be out of reach from every direction. I glanced over at Jenn. Two of the nightmare-wolves sniffed around the outside of her cage, lifted their heads, decided to leave her alone for the time being, and came over to join the others at mine.

They surrounded me. They sniffed and snorted at the cage, pressed their noses in between the branches and scared the shit out of me. It was the most uncomfortable I've felt in my entire life. They couldn't reach me, but they were too close for me to feel safe. My heart raced. I wanted them to go away. My stomach clenched and I felt like I was going to puke. Even after all of my dealings with Mr. Nightmare, I had never understood the phrase 'sick with fear' when I read about it in horror books. I could never empathize with the feeling. Until the nightmare-wolves had me surrounded. I hoped they would realize they couldn't get to me, get bored, and leave.

My hopes did nothing however, because the more they sniffed around my cage, the more agitated they became. Soon, instead of just sniffing and growling at me, they were barking and yelping. It was a loud bark, short, sharp, and intense from some of them, while others howled and yelped, a sound more reminiscent of a hyena than a dog.

At each bark, I jumped, until it became so loud in the cage I couldn't distinguish between one bark and the next. I was trapped in the center of a busy hive of noise and aggression. It was impossible to keep an eye on them all at the same time. The cage filled with the odor of raw meat and the sour smell of old rotting leaves— the overwhelming and insidious smell of decay and death.

It felt like they were there for hours, barking and howling, waiting for their next meal to be made available for them.

I balled up in the middle of the cage and buried my head between my knees so I wouldn't have to look at their faces. The only thoughts I let in my head were positive ones. I tried to push everything else to the side. With my eyes closed, I sat and tried to put myself into a sort of meditation designed to remove me from the stress of the situation. I thought of home, of my family, my friends; I thought of good times with Chuck and of time spent working with Jenn before the stress of the last few days. It worked; for a few wonderful moments I couldn't hear the barks or smell the terrible breath of the beasts around me. It was almost as if I'd left my cage.

"Okay, okay." A confident and familiar voice ripped through

the barking and interrupted my positive thoughts. "Come here, come here."

I looked up when the barking stopped and saw the night-mare-wolves stroll casually over to John who stood at the entrance to the hallway. They gathered on either side of him and behind him, no longer looking like wild animals, instead looking up at him, mouths mostly closed, tails wagging like a pack of perfectly trained dogs. John reached down and patted one on the head. A second one leaned in for some attention, and John patted that one too.

"You're always full of surprises, Anna," John said. He bent again and scratched a third nightmare-wolf under the chin. He strolled toward my tree-cage and the pack followed him, staying either behind him or off to his side. "I thought you might try to reach in and take my dreams like we did to Mr. Nightmare all those years ago, but I didn't think you'd just jump right through. It was pretty smart of you to figure all of that out."

I didn't say anything; I kept my mouth shut and watched as he approached. When he got to my cage, he stood at the wooden bars and grabbed the branches while the nightmare-wolves gathered and then sat behind him. He looked the cage up and down, examining it.

"What do you want with me, John?" I asked. My voice was low. I couldn't hide my fear and didn't want to. This place had a hand in the death of my brother; I knew what I was facing and my chances at survival were slim. The only thing keeping me going was the fact that Jenn could still get home. She wasn't really involved in any of it. She wanted to help a friend and got pulled in—I pulled her in, and I would pull her out too. I'd get her home even if I had to stay.

He snorted through his nose.

"It's funny to hear you call me by name, you know. It was strange the other day when you used it, and I still haven't gotten used to it," he said. His tone was relaxed, almost like the boy I used to know. Almost.

"What do you go by now?" I was genuinely curious.

Wind whipped sand in my face and I flinched away from it. John didn't move; he kept his face against the branches of my cage and peered in, his hat keeping his face in the shadows.

"They make up names for us. Mr. Nightmare, the boogeyman, the monster under the bed, whatever kids can think of to call us. Mr. Nightmare is just what we called him. His real name is Arthur Middleton. We called him Mr. Nightmare and it stuck. It doesn't really matter what our names are. We do the same thing. We eat dreams, Anna." John still hadn't moved and I felt the anxiety and fear rising again in my chest. I couldn't be still. I wanted to get out of there and felt like I was going to puke if I didn't get up and move. My stomach was a tight knot, my legs weak and shaky; tears were about to pour from my eyes once more. I paced back and forth as best I could, rocking my weight from one foot to the other, anything to move my body and release some tension. I wanted to scream.

"Why do this to me, then?" I said. "I was fine. I graduated college, I had a job and was doing great on my own. Get your dreams from somewhere else. Leave me and Merrie and Marcus alone. You're still our friend and we will always love you, John. There's no reason to do this."

"Yes, there is, Anna-B," he shouted and slammed his hands against the branches shaking the entire cage. He spoke again, quieter, calmer, "Yes, there is. You set me up. All three of you set me up to take the fall. You said you'd do it, but in your head, you knew I wouldn't let you. You *knew* I was the best athlete and if anyone could get close to Mr. Nightmare to take those dreams, it would be me. You knew going inside him led to this place because you'd been here. You knew I'd do anything for Chuckie. Anything. You *knew* what would happen, Anna, and you let me do it anyway. I'm stronger now—as strong as Mr. Nightmare was when he came to see us before—and I want you to be stuck here. I can't go back, but you can stay here with me. You and Merrie and Marcus. Then we can have a *real* Nightmare Club. Kids will sleep in your world every night and the four of us can go out together, gorge ourselves and devour their dreams. It will be like old times, Anna. But better."

"It wasn't like that, John, it never..." I started, but he stopped me before I got the chance to continue.

"I don't care anymore about the past, Anna," he snapped. The nightmare-wolves perked up at this, and all of them began to pace back and forth around the outside of my cage. None of them took their eyes off me. "I really don't. You asked me why, so I told you why. But I've moved on from then. I'm a different person now. A better person. Which is why I'm going to offer you a deal. I don't want just you here, Anna. I want all of us here. So, your friend over there stays here. You'll go back down the hallway and into your world. Collect Merrie and Marcus and bring them back here. I know you, Anna. I know you're thinking mostly about getting your friend home safe. This is your chance. All three of you come back, and I'll let her go home, unhurt, and no one will ever bother her again. If you don't, then I'll keep her here. Or maybe I'll feed her to my dogs —they don't eat dreams and they get hungry you know." When he spoke about the dogs, they stopped pacing and looked up at him. Then, in unison, they all began pacing again.

John said something low and unintelligible under his breath. I couldn't make out what it was, but it didn't matter, I got the gist right away. The nightmare-wolves left my cage and trotted over to Jenn's. Like they had done with mine, they encircled it, snarling, teeth bared and heads down, ready to pounce at a moment's notice—or a single word from their master.

Jenn screamed over the snarls and howls. I don't know if she'd been asleep or simply not paying attention to what was going on, but it took her by surprise.

"Don't worry," I shouted, unsure if she could hear me. "I'm going to take care of you."

John wiggled two fingers and the branches holding me in parted, creating an opening.

"Let's go," John said. He stood right in front of the opening. I didn't want to get too close, but if I was going to get out of this, I knew I had to. I walked fast, right toward him, keeping my eyes down at the ground. He didn't back away fast enough and my shoulder brushed up against his arm. I kept walking, doing my best to make him believe I was angry, when I was actually feeling a little hopeful inside. I might have figured out a way to give us a chance.

The hopeful feeling was short-lived. I didn't want Jenn to think I had abandoned her so I began to walk toward her cage. John shouted something in a language I didn't understand. Two short quick words and then a third. Two of the nightmare-wolves lifted their heads, turned and looked at John, then shifted their gaze to me. I backpedaled a step and then two more as they galloped toward me. And, like before, their heads were down, ready to attack.

"Okay," I said, and took a few more steps toward the hall-way. "Okay, John."

I continued my movement toward the hall, but I refused to turn my back on the creatures coming at me. They bared their teeth and barked at me, first one then the other.

"Go inside and I'll call them off," John said. "I need to come with you, but it can just be the two of us, or my two friends can come with us if you want."

"I'm going," I said, and continued backward into the open mouth of the hall. I stopped when I was completely inside with wood on all four sides of me. John said something else to the nightmare-wolves and they gave me a final look before leaving. I couldn't see Jenn's cage from where I stood, but I assumed they joined the rest of the wolves there. A few seconds later, John came inside.

"Ready," he said. "Let's do this." For a second it felt like we were on the same side again. Even after everything he'd done, I still had a hard time thinking of John as anyone other than my friend. I wanted so bad for him to realize the error of his ways and be on my side again like when we were kids. When he spoke, I could hear him saying it as a kid before we did something together, and it made me hopeful once more that he would change his ways. He moved past me with ease and I followed him into the darkness.

"Stop," John said after we'd walked for a while down the hallway. I halted my progress immediately. I couldn't see much in front of me. John was far enough ahead that I didn't know exactly where he was, though I could hear his footsteps from inside the dark.

"Sorry to do this to you," John said. I could tell by the tone of voice he wasn't sorry at all. He was happy and excited about whatever was about to happen. In an instant, the darkness around us vanished. Light flooded in all around us, as if the walls, floor and ceiling were glowing. The sudden burst of light made me slam my eyes shut; I held my hand over them and waited. Eventually, I squinted and let my eyes adjust to the light. I kept my gaze down at the ground though, knowing I still couldn't allow myself to see John's face. There was pressure at my back. I tried to turn but two strong, vice-like hands wrapped around my shoulders. John was still in front of me and knew whose arms had coiled themselves around me.

"Time to open those eyes, Anna-banana," Mr. Nightmare spoke right into my ear. He put one arm across my chest as I struggled, turning one way then the other trying to get out of his grip. I thrashed back and forth, his hold only tightening. I couldn't move.

"Not worth fighting," Mr. Nightmare said. My nose filled with the rotting stench of his breath. "Now, open those eyes,"

He held me in place with a single arm and his hand came up to my forehead. He put two fingers just above my eyelids and jerked my head back even as I fought to keep it pointed down at the ground.

"No use in fighting, Anna," John said. "Open up."

I squeezed my eyes shut, but Mr. Nightmare put two fingers right on the lids again and forced them open. I was helpless in his grasp. He pried my eyelids open even wider. I screamed as his hand moved from my shoulders to my chin. I couldn't move or twist away without risking breaking my neck, because he wasn't going to let my head move an inch. He tilted my head back and forced my gaze in John's direction. My former friend removed his hat and pushed the hair out of his face.

The brightened hallway spun. I couldn't look away. Mr. Nightmare held me there as my stomach churned. Both of them laughed; I could hear it echoing around me even as the world drifted away. My pants got warm and wet. Burning bile rose from my stomach through my esophagus and filled my mouth. Everything went dark.

CHAPTER 27

I awoke amid rubble and the remains of the farmhouse. It was daytime, though I didn't know what day. There was no sign of Merrie, Marcus, or Marcus's car. I wasn't on the second floor anymore, because there was no second floor. Three of the four first-floor walls were missing. Pieces of wood and shingles were everywhere. My head rested on a board that looked as though it had once been part of the siding, a rusted nail poking out only a few inches from my face. I rolled away from the nail and onto my stomach, then pushed myself up to get a better view. The day was clear and sunny, and without most of the walls of the house around me, I could see the path the tornado took as it came through the fields. It hit the farmhouse head-on before continuing through the field on the other side. I'd seen Mr. Nightmare control the weather before, and the thought ran through my head that the tornado might have been sent for the farmhouse on purpose.

There was no sign of Merrie or Marcus—probably a good thing. They had been okay the last time Jenn saw them, and the lack of Marcus's car meant they probably left once the storm had passed and it didn't look like either of us were coming back through to this side.

My head pounded; the usual feeling of a severe hangover rushed through my body. I got to my feet and looked out over the empty fields. My first thought being, why weren't there any emergency vehicles here, or someone checking on the damage? I got up, stumbled out of the farmhouse—looking out for more stray, rusted nails— and down the dirt driveway to the main road. I'd never hitchhiked, but I considered it. My head throbbed and it was hard to keep my eyes open. My muscles ached; I smelled like piss. In the end, I decided just to start walking. If I couldn't make it, I'd find a pay phone somewhere and call Merrie or Marcus collect—or even my parents if I had to—and get a ride home.

After what felt like an incredibly longtime walking, I'd made it almost a third of the way home, but still had about ten miles of walking left to do. My body felt better and despite my extreme thirst, I wasn't sore and my muscles felt strong enough to move a little faster. I picked up my pace and broke into a jog. I didn't have my music and I wasn't in my regular running clothes, but they'd still be considered gym clothes by most. I knew I could run home. It was hot—though not as hot as it had been before the storm—and I started sweating pretty good. At first, my head pounded with every footfall. I kept pushing forward, keeping a steady pace throughout the run. Soon the pounding in my head stopped and I was feeling as good as I'd felt on any run I'd been on the entire summer. It was as if the hangover feeling was coming out in my sweat. I passed a few pay phones but kept running as home got closer. I'd be there in no time.

When I finally turned into the Prairie View neighborhood, I was starting to worry more about Merrie and Marcus. The car wasn't at the farm. I'd assumed it meant they'd left and were all right. But the run—without music—gave me time to think. If the tornado destroyed the farmhouse, it wouldn't be out of the realm of possibility that it had flung the car somewhere else.

And if it flung a car, well, then it wouldn't be hard to do the same to my friends.

I'd been gone a long time in this world and I knew my parents would be worried about me, but a quick check on Merrie wouldn't take long, so I ran past my house—both my parents' cars were in the driveway—and kept running down the street to Merrie's house.

Her car wasn't there, but it was most likely still with the police or at the shop, so I slowed to a walk as I approached. I walked up the driveway, still breathing heavy and sweating, and rang the doorbell.

I heard movement inside the house and saw a shadow moving through the curtained front door window, but I couldn't tell who was inside. The door opened and I looked into Merrie's bruised face.

"Holy shit," we both said at the same time.

"Come in," Merrie said, almost in a whisper, and waved me into the house.

I went in and she looked up and down either side of the street before shutting the door.

"What the fuck happened?" I said as soon as she turned around.

Merrie smiled. "Anna, I could ask the same about you. Where the hell have you been?"

"You go first," I said. "How long has it been?"

"Three days." Merrie waved me into the living room to sit. "Your parents have been searching everywhere, making phone calls and talking about getting the police involved. Luckily, they haven't yet."

I was speechless. Time had obviously passed differently here, or maybe I hadn't realized how long I'd sat in that cage before John set me free.

"What happened after I left?" I said.

"Short version?" Merrie said. "You jumped into John a second or two before a tornado hit the house. We dove to the ground, and when Jenn dove, John kinda moved toward her like he wanted her to fall inside of him or whatever happens there. Then John disappeared a few seconds later. The roof ripped off the house and we got downstairs into a doorway before the rest of the house came apart. We waited a few hours; when neither of you came back we knew we had to leave because there were sirens and stuff everywhere."

"Shit, the bruises are from the tornado?" I asked, reaching out and touching the side of her face gently. She winced.

"Yeah, rough couple of days for me here. Drove through a wall then got hit by a tornado." Merrie shrugged. Her mouth turned down and she started to cry. I went to her and wrapped my arms around her. He pressed her face into my shoulder, but she pulled away in obvious pain and switched to the other side. We stood there for a long time, and I let her cry. I started crying too. I didn't know what we were going to do and I had no answers. Things weren't getting easier. My shirt was already damp from sweat, was soaked where her face had been. She looked at me and wiped her eyes. I did the same, smearing the tears away with the heel of my palm.

"Sorry," Merrie said. "What happened to you?"

I relayed the story as best I could, telling her every detail as it came to mind.

"Holy shit." Merrie stared at me when I was finished.

"There's one more thing," I said. "John and Mr. Nightmare, they want me to bring you guys back. You and Marcus. They said it was the only way they were going to let Jenn go. John knows me too well; even if Mr. Nightmare warped his mind to believe that I knew all along he'd end up stuck there, he still remembers enough about me to know I wouldn't leave a friend behind."

Merrie nodded. "He knows you're going to come back and try to help her, so he doesn't care if you leave. He doesn't need you to stay if he has your friend. But you don't really think he believes that bullshit about you knowing all along what would happen to him, or that you orchestrated it somehow."

"I think he's not even the same person, Merrie." I got up because I knew I couldn't stay. I had to let my parents know I was okay. "He has John's memories but they're foggy and warped. He's not the kid we knew. Maybe Mr. Nightmare wasn't really a bad guy either until he went there. Something there changes you. I have to get Jenn out. There's one more thing, too. When I left, I brushed past John. I made contact with him. His voice was different there than it is here. He's solid there. He might have magic or special powers or something. But he was also solid. If he's solid, I think we can hurt him."

Merrie sighed. "Where have I heard that before?"

"I know." I shrugged. "I have to go home, but I know I'm right this time. He was solid. I couldn't stick my hand in him. Mr. Nightmare grabbed me and I leaned back against him. We can't do that here because they're like conduits or something to the Nightmare Realm. I think we can hurt them there, in the Nightmare Realm."

"Let's talk," Merrie said. "Go see your parents. Make up a story like you always do. Then we can figure it out, like *we* always do."

"Sounds like a plan," I said. "Before I go, what did you tell people, so I know for my story?"

"We said we were out by the farm—just the two of us—and the siren went off so we figured the farmhouse would be a good place for shelter. Ended up being a bad spot."

It sounded like a plausible story to me. Merrie was right, we always figured something out when our backs were against the wall, and with every passing second the need to help Jenn became more urgent. She couldn't wait a long time for us. If what we thought was true, her mind was being warped every second she was there. If we waited too long, she wouldn't be the same person when we got there. We needed to do it soon.

CHAPTER 28

I walked the short distance to my house. I didn't really have a story in mind when I got there, most of my mental energy was being used trying to figure out how to get Jenn back. I needed to be home, needed to slow everything down for a few minutes and get ready to go back, so I pushed open the front door and decided to wing it. The good news was I was technically an adult and I didn't need to check in with my parents every day; the bad news was they called around looking for me, so I couldn't completely control the story because other people were involved. Hopefully, once I got home, the worry about me would be easily forgotten and no one would look into my story too much. There was also Jenn's disappearance to account for.

"Mom," I called as soon as the front door swung open. "Dad!"

"Anna," their voices answered at almost the exact same time from the back of the house. They were in their bedroom. I heard the movement even as I walked down the hall toward them.

"Anna," Mom said again when she came around the corner from the kitchen. Her eyes were red, but there was a huge smile on her face. In my horror books I sometimes read about worry melting off of someone's face. I saw it then. When Mom came around the corner and saw me standing there, her face changed. I watched it happen and understood how hard it had been for them.

"Hey, Mom," I said. I felt a sense of relief I wasn't expecting. As if being at home with Mom and Dad pulled away an anxiety I didn't know was there. She came to me and wrapped her arms around me. I hugged her back.

"Hey, kiddo," Dad said, and hugged both of us there in the doorway between the hall and the kitchen.

I knew they had a million questions and eventually I'd have to answer them.

"I'm so glad you're okay." Mom hugged me tight to her chest again.

"I am," I said. Then I started to weave a tale. "I wanted to get in touch with you."

"Where were you?" Dad asked. He looked at me over Mom's head.

"So, I've been trying to stretch out my runs a little bit more. More miles per day and I wanted to see how far I could go if I kept running. I ended up a few towns over when it started raining. I didn't know the storm was going to be so bad. Then the tornado siren went off. There were no buildings around so I kept running and watching the sky. I ended up in some woods. I got turned around and finally found my way out. I'm a little hungry and dirty and tired, but other than that, no worse for wear."

"You weren't with Jenn?" Dad asked.

I did my best to look surprised. I knew the question was coming, so I was prepared.

"No, why?" I said.

"Jenn's been missing since the tornado, too." Mom said.

"We assumed you were together," Dad added.

I shook my head, still doing the best acting job I could. "No, I saw her before the storm and she said she was going back to check on the restaurant since she was supposed to work that night. No one has seen her?"

"No," Dad said. "We were actually less worried because she wasn't showing up either. We figured wherever you were, you were with her. We called her dad, and when he said she hadn't been home after the storm we just assumed…well, I'm just glad you're okay."

"Yeah." I said. "I'm fine. Tired and hungry, but fine. Really. Now worried about Jenn too. Maybe she'll turn up soon too."

None of what I told them was a lie. I *was* worried about Jenn and I hoped she'd turn up soon. Though, if that was going to happen, I was going to have to be involved in her rescue.

Once everything had slowed down, I realized how hungry I was—especially after running home. Mom started making me food: eggs and bacon with toast. I was so excited for it my hands were shaking, but I couldn't wait. I went to the cupboard and made myself of bowl of cereal but told Mom to keep cooking because I was going to want more. Mom had whole milk in the fridge she usually used for cooking, so I added it and cereal to a bowl and ate it all, then I drank the milk right out of the bowl. I repeated the process and finished the second bowl as Mom was getting the eggs and bacon out of the pan. I started eating right away. When all the food was gone my hands were still a little shaky, but my stomach felt full and I sat at the table until the food was digested enough to reset my blood sugar or whatever was going on with the shaking. About ten minutes later I felt more or less like myself. I stayed for a bit because Mom wanted to talk. She'd been worried and was glad I was home, so I didn't mind talking to her for a bit, but I could feel the exhaustion catching up with me. My whole body felt like it was being tugged down to the floor. I had to get up.

I left the kitchen, went right into the bathroom, and took a shower. If I'd stopped anywhere and sat, I would have fallen asleep. The hot water felt good. Even though it was the middle of summer, I felt like I couldn't get the water turned up hot enough. I needed to burn the feeling of the Nightmare Realm from my body, as if taking away every piece of skin that had been there would somehow erase it from my memory. Part of me wished I could. For a split second the idea crossed my mind of leaving Jenn there. I'd never have to go back. I could leave Illinois—maybe move to California or something—and she would never be able to find me, even if she became like Mr. Nightmare and was able to come through to our world. The thought was short-lived. I'd feel guilty for the rest of my life and never be able to live with myself. The hot water became lukewarm, so I got out of the shower, ran a brush through my hair, then wrapped myself in a towel and crossed the hall to my room.

Despite my thoughts in the shower, every second that passed felt like I was abandoning Jenn. She was stuck there and I was here, eating bacon and eggs and taking a shower. She was there in a cage with angry nightmare-wolves frothing at the mouth and barking in her face. She wasn't getting food or water or a shower, so why should I? I sat down on my bed with the intention to make a plan for how to get her back. Mr. Nightmare and John were different there. Their bodies were solid. They didn't act like portals to the other side like when they did here. I needed to come up with a way to hurt them. I laid back on my bed, still wrapped in my towel. My eyes had closed before I realized what happened.

I woke up three hours later.

CHAPTER 29

The sound of Mom knocking gently at my door woke me. My eyes snapped open. It had been a dreamless sleep—I don't think I could have handled the nightmares if it wasn't. I was instantly worried. Worried about Jenn. Worried I'd slept for too long and there was no longer a way to get her back, at least not the way I remembered her. I sat up in bed and pulled the towel around me.

"Anna," Mom said.

"Yeah, Mom," I said as I fumbled to get dressed. I couldn't stay. I needed to find Merrie and Marcus and get Jenn back. "One second."

"Merrie called to see if there was any news," Mom said through the door. "I told her you were home so she is coming to visit. I hope that's okay."

"Oh. Yeah. That's great. I'm getting dressed, I'll be out in a second." I got up and finished putting on my clothes. I put my hair up then went out to the living room. I'd managed to clear my head for a few hours thanks to the nap, but once I was awake my thoughts began to race once again. Merrie knew I was back so was she coming because she hadn't heard from me or because she was with Marcus. Maybe she'd talked to him.

My mind kept wandering from one possibility to the next. I wanted to know what Merrie needed. Or what Marcus had to say. I wanted to know what Mr. Nightmare and John had in mind for us, or for Jenn. There was too much to think about and I was stuck in a loop, unable to focus on one thing for very long. I had to calm myself down and wait until Merrie got there so we could figure this shit out together.

I made small talk with Mom in the living room while the TV played in the background. I tried to give reasonable answers to her questions. She was obviously worried, but I had too much on my mind to have the conversation she wanted. Thankfully, I didn't have to wait long. I looked out the large picture window and saw Merrie walking with a slight limp up our driveway. I wondered why she hadn't driven over, then remembered her driving through the front window of the bar. It had been a long week. The look on her face told me something was wrong before she even got to the front door.

I got up and opened the door for her. Mom stood behind me and greeted my friend, asking about Merrie's injures and how she was holding up mentally after the accident. Merrie, too nice to tell Mom we needed to talk in private, gave her answers that would make her happy.

"I'll let you girls talk," Mom said after the small talk was done, and she disappeared back into the house. I sat on the top step of the front porch and Merrie joined me. We sat with our shoulders touching, looking down at the ground like two spies in a movie trying to make it appear like they weren't having a conversation.

"Something's wrong," I said, my voice low in case Mom was still able to hear us. It wasn't a question, I knew my friend well enough to know when things weren't right.

"Marcus is gone," she said. Her face was serious and there was a slight waver in her voice.

"What? What do you mean?" I put my arm around her, my hand on her shoulder, because even if she was overreacting—

completely possible given the situation—she *believed* something was wrong, which was enough for me to want to comfort her.

"He went to work this morning, like regular. We didn't know when, or if, you were coming back, so it was easier to go on with life and then switch things up, obviously, when you showed back up," she said. I nodded. It wasn't what I wanted to hear, but I understood what she was saying; there was no way for them to know if I was ever coming back. It had been a couple days already and they couldn't sit around the old farmhouse—the remnants of it—and wait for me. They didn't have a choice. We moved on when John left us for the Nightmare Realm; they had to act as if I was gone or missing, and hope I came back.

"He went to work today," Merrie continued. "We said we'd call each other right away if anything changed. After you left, I called his office and the receptionist said he wasn't there. That's happened before so I didn't think anything of it, maybe he was on a break or just not at his cubicle. I'd try again later. I waited a couple hours and called again. She said after I called the first time, she'd asked around. He was at work, someone had seen him looking out the window, then he left in a rush and seemed to be very upset. She asked me if there was something going on that I knew about—she must have known we're together or something because I've talked to her a few times. I told her there was nothing going on as far as I knew. When I hung up, I called his apartment—there was no answer. I called his parents too, to see if maybe he'd talked to them, but it had been a few days since they'd talked to him."

"Okay," I said. I had to stay calm because if I acted like things were out of control, it would only increase Merrie's anxiety. Marcus must have seen something outside his office. "We don't know he's missing for sure. Only that he left work upset."

She gave me a familiar look. Merrie could tell I was feeding her bullshit to make her feel better, and the look made it obvious she wasn't buying it. She needed honesty from me, not a protector.

"All right," I said. "Listen, I know how it looks. Given the amount of shit we've had going on, there isn't really another way to look at it. They came after me on my run. They came after you in your car. They showed up at his job once already, and now they might have done it a second time. But we don't know for sure. We can drive over to his office and try to find him. Check his place and then…" I stopped talking because I was thinking about another trip to the farm. When we saw Mr. Nightmare as kids, our Dwelling—where we told the stories every week—was the focal point of Mr. Nightmare and his power. For whatever reason, the focal point had shifted. Maybe the Dwelling was another one of those places where the curtain between the worlds was thin. Maybe they could *only* pass into our world at the farm and then move around easily once they were here. There was too much we still didn't know about them.

"You know we're going to end up back there," Merrie said. I nodded and got up.

"You ready now?" I said.

"No," she sighed. "But we don't really have a choice, right? If Marcus is here, we need him to get Jenn back. If he's there, well, then, we have to go get both of them."

"Yup," I said. I climbed up the steps and went back into the house. I'd been missing for two days and was about to leave again. I hoped when I told them I'd be back soon, I was actually going to be back soon. What would it do to them if I disappeared for another two days? Or forever? They already had to deal with Chuck's death; if I died or disappeared forever it would devastate them all over again. I had to push those thoughts from my head. My friends came first.

"Hey, Mom," I called into the house as I grabbed my purse and keys. I hesitated, remembering the sewing shears ten years earlier, then I took a knife out of the block on the counter and slipped in into the back pocket of my jeans. "I'm going out with Merrie for a bit! I'll be back later."

I turned and walked back to the front door without stopping, knowing Mom would be coming along to make sure I was feeling okay. I made it almost to the driver's side of the Dying Buffalo when the front door squeaked open.

"Anna," Mom said. "You sure you're feeling okay?"

"Yeah," I said and smiled. I turned so she wouldn't see the knife in the back of my pants. "I'll be back soon."

"Okay," Mom said. "Take care of her, Merrie!"

Merrie gave her a wave and Mom ducked her head back into the house. I turned on the car, looked over at Merrie, and we both nodded. With our plan and final destination set, I backed the car out of the driveway and we were off.

CHAPTER 30

The first place we checked was Marcus's office. He was supposed to be there and we wanted to rule it out. The first thing we noticed was the spot Marcus had parked his car in the last time we were there was empty. Marcus was a creature of habit and he would have parked in the same spot, or as close to the same spot as he could get. Maybe he parked somewhere else, so we checked the whole lot. His car wasn't there. We walked around the building and didn't see any sign of him. He didn't smoke, but we checked the smoke break area too. Instead of going up to the second floor where he worked, Merrie used the pay phone in the lobby and called upstairs to the office; she held the receiver out to the side so we could both listen. The same receptionist she'd talked to before answered and said no one had seen Marcus since he left in a rush; he hadn't even told his boss he was leaving. According to the woman, who had talked to others at the office, he'd been looking out the window at nothing in particular, seemed to get really upset about something, and then stormed out of the office; it was very unlike him. Merrie thanked her and hung up the phone.

"I think they can make themselves visible to some people but not to everyone," Merrie said.

"Like Chuck's wake," I said. "No one else could see Mr. Nightmare, but the four of us could."

"He wasn't looking out there at nothing." Merrie pointed through the glass door of the building to the small forest preserve across the street, assuming Marcus had seen Mr. Nightmare and John there a few days earlier. "He was looking at *them*. Christ, I hope he didn't run across the street and try to confront those two."

"That's probably what happened, or something like it," I said. "Let's check his place and see what we can find out. If he's not there we'll go to the farm again and end this, one way or the other."

Merrie agreed. We were at Marcus's place thirty minutes later. At his apartment building, his assigned parking spot was empty. Merrie sighed when we pulled in. She wanted to get to the farm as soon as possible.

"A quick check," I said. "Then we'll go. You have a key?"

"Yeah." Merrie held up a set of keys. We went in and up to his place. Merrie unlocked the door and went in first. I followed behind her.

"Marcus," she called as soon as she entered. I knew he wouldn't be there, but at least it was hopeful thinking. Merrie went down the hall right away toward the bedroom, and I walked into the kitchen. My attention went first to the stove because there was a pan on it, as if maybe Marcus really *was* there and had just finished cooking an egg or something. Then I noticed a piece of paper on the counter addressed to Merrie.

I started to read it but Merrie came out of the bedroom shaking her head.

"He left you a note," I said, pointing down at the counter. Merrie came over next to me and we read it together.

Mer, I don't want anything to happen to you. I'm going back to the farm. Maybe I can try to reason with John. I don't know. We used to be good friends. I can make him understand. He'd never actually want to hurt Anna. I will get her and Jenn back. Please don't come looking for me. I need to know you're safe. I love you. Marcus.

"Fuck," Merrie said when she was done. I read it again. He hadn't called her because he knew she'd try to stop him. He wanted to do this on his own for Jenn and I, but mostly for Merrie. Marcus didn't want anything to happen to her, and the only way he could be certain nothing happened to her was to go there and take care of things himself.

"We knew we were going back anyway," I said. "Now it looks like we have two people to save instead of one. Remember, for as fucked up as John's head is right now, he still only wants one thing: the Nightmare Club back together. He's not going to hurt Marcus because there'd be no more club then. Jenn, on the other hand, is more dispensable now. He knows we'll come back for Marcus. He doesn't need two hostages."

"You're probably right," Merrie said. "Let's go."

Merrie took a step to the door but I reached out and grabbed her arm.

"Wait." I pulled her back toward me, then went into the kitchen again. I pulled open the drawers and found Marcus's steak knives, then held one up to Merrie. "Take it."

"Come on," she said. "This is supernatural shit. We can't just go in there with a couple of steak knives." Despite her words, she took the knife from me.

"Not the best weapon, but right now, we don't have anything else," I said. "We need protection. Even if it's to slow down those nightmare-wolves. It's better than nothing."

Merrie grinned at me and it reminded me of the attitude she always had whenever Mr. Nightmare used to show up. She held the knife in her hand looking a little like Michael Meyers, looking for someone to slice up.

"Try to be a little more discreet," I said as we left the apartment. Merrie cupped the knife handle and held the blade against her arm so it wouldn't be so obvious.

"Like this?" she said.

"Much better," I said. "One last time?"

"I hope so…" Merrie's mouth tightened, and she locked up Marcus's place. Then we left and made one final trip to the Shaw Farm.

CHAPTER 31

I turned the Dying Buffalo onto the farm's dirt driveway. The old car shimmied and rattled over the uneven road, the roar of the thing announcing our arrival.

Merrie's face had gone serious the moment we got in the car at Marcus's place. I knew she was ready for whatever happened.

"If Marcus is already there and we show up," I said, "they'll be ready for us. They will take us and try to do...I don't know, whatever their plan for us is. They might even let Jenn go if they really have no use for her. I don't know, but if the three of us are there, Mr. Nightmare and John will have exactly what they wanted."

"Yeah." Merrie flashed the knife in front of her as I pulled the car in behind the destroyed house and put it in park. "If they want to come at us, we go at them. I just hope these things work. We have no choice; we have to go get them."

John and Mr. Nightmare had powers and we didn't even know everything they could do. We thought we'd defeated Mr. Nightmare before but now he was back, and he had help with him this time. There was still so much we didn't know about the nightmare-people and the Realm. There was no telling what would happen there. We couldn't leave our friends though. The only thing we could control was what we were going to do when we got there. We could listen to John and Mr. Nightmare and submit ourselves to whatever it was they wanted, or we could fight back and try like hell to bring Jenn and Marcus home. It had been a long road, but when we got out of the Dying Buffalo, it felt like the final standoff. The Nightmare Club would come face-to-face with Mr. Nightmare one last time.

"Let's do this," I said and got out of the car. We both slammed our doors at the same time and then walked around to where the stairs up to the front porch had once been.

We stepped through the rubble gingerly. Neither of us had boots on and there was a plethora of dirty, rusted nails poking up in random spots and lots of broken glass as well. A few of the shards from the windows stuck up at odd angles. As we waded through the maze of sharp wood, nails, and glass I was surprised by the fact I was able to make it out of this place without getting cut earlier in the day.

"I guess we stand about where that room was." Merrie said what'd I'd been thinking. We looked up into the sky as if imagining the house standing there above us, then walked to the correct corner—as close as we could get to the room without having a ladder to get us up in the air. Wind blew across the field. There was the fresh scent of vegetation and fertile soil. A huge swath of corn had been ripped up by the tornado, but most of it remained. The sun beat down on us and we stood, unmoving, in the exact right spot. Merrie flexed her hand around the knife and I lifted up my shirt and grabbed my knife as well. I palmed it like her, keeping the blade flat against my forearm. It didn't make the knife invisible, but it made the thing harder to see.

"Hey John," Merrie shouted. "You wanted the Nightmare Club? Here we fucking are! Come on and get us."

The wind whipped again across the field and I knew it wasn't a random breeze. None of the events that took place on the farm were random. The tornado, the hail, the wind, everything had a purpose.

"There's the little bitch." A voice came from all around us. It wasn't John's voice, though. It was Mr. Nightmare. I felt him right behind us and turned slowly, eyes to the ground, to see him there, towering over us. Merrie tensed next to me; I gripped the knife tighter in my hand, keeping it pressed to my arm. I didn't want him to see my weapon here, where an attack would do us no good. We needed to wait until we were in the Nightmare Realm. It would help if John was with him too so we could get them both at the same time. Merrie and I hadn't mentioned it beforehand, but I hope she'd thought of it.

"Well," Merrie said. "We're here. You want us all together, right? Let Jenn go and bring us to Marcus."

"You're right," Mr. Nightmare hissed. His speech was slow, each word drawn out as though he was enjoying this and wanted to make us wait. "I do want to see my beloved Nightmare Club back together again. Young Jonathan has become quite the apprentice to me. It doesn't matter how old Marcus gets, he will always be nothing but a scared boy in my eyes. Just as *you* will always be a little bitch. And Anna-banana? Well, we know what Anna-banana thinks about my friend John. We knew she'd come running once she got the chance to talk to the love of her life. We only needed to get her and we knew the two of you would come with her. She's the one that runs the whole thing even if you don't realize it. Anna always gets her way, don't you, Anna?"

My face tightened. The urge to rush at him was strong but I held it at bay. Not yet. Not yet.

"And what about Jenn?" I said, my voice shaking with anger. "You have any remarkable observations about her?"

"No," Mr. Nightmare said in a dismissive tone. His hand waved at the air next to him. The brim of his top hat hid his face. "I think she might make a fun toy for the pups, though. Don't you think?"

I didn't need to see his face to know he was smiling.

"I think it's time we go," he said. I started to take a step toward him, ready to attack him and John in their own world. I'd only ever entered the Realm though John so I assumed we'd go through Mr. Nightmare the same way. I wasn't looking forward to the frigid feeling worming its way into my bones. But the feeling was momentary; getting a chance to kill Mr. Nightmare a second time would be worth it. I'd even stare into his terrifying, indescribable face as I watched him die.

"Oh." He raised a hand and I stopped. "We are missing one member of the Nightmare Club, aren't we? Where is Chuck? Have you seen him lately, Anna-banana?"

My hand shook and I made a move to charge at Mr. Nightmare. His laugh echoed around us and throughout the entire farm. Merrie grabbed my arm and pulled me back.

"Not yet," she said, softly into my ear. She held me tight and wouldn't let me get any closer to him. I screamed as loud as I could, drowning out the evil laugh of my long-time tormentor.

"Let's fucking go then." Merrie spat the words at him. "Enough of this bullshit. Do what you're going to do, or get the fuck out of here."

"I'll do what I want, when I want, little bitch," Mr. Nightmare said. His tone had changed on a dime. Instead of joking and having fun with us, he was angry. Maybe Merrie had gotten to him. "But you're right. The time for fun is over. Let's get on with this."

Without warning he reached for us, both at the same time. The coldness of his hand wrapped around my throat. He was fast. I didn't have time to react. He did the same to Merrie, grabbing her by the neck before he pulled us toward him. His tall body rushed toward me and I couldn't stop myself. The coldness spread from my neck to my face and chest, then to my arms and legs. He pulled us inside himself, into the darkness. Dreams surrounded me once more and we were there, inside the Nightmare Realm.

CHAPTER 32

When I went through last time—under my own power—I landed gently on my feet upon entering this other place. The second time, I'd been forced through the portal between worlds and I crashed hard into the ground, then collapsed to my knees. My hands slammed into the dirt. Merrie fell down next to me, landing flat on her chest. I could hear the air puff out of her lungs at she made contact. I got up to my knees and reached for her as she rolled onto her side. She gasped for breath and grabbed her chest. She coughed and sucked at the air.

"It's okay," I said, keeping my voice low and putting a hand on her back. "You got the wind knocked out of you. Lay there a minute and relax your breathing, it will come back slow. The more you relax, the sooner you'll catch your breath." Merrie must have had the wind knocked out of her at some point in her life, at least using how hard we played as kids as a reference, but I also knew that when it happened, having someone there to talk to you and keep you calm usually helped, because getting the wind knocked out of you felt like you were about to die.

Just as Merrie's breathing started to slow down and she was able to get herself up on her knees, there was a noise behind us, deeper inside the underground hallway.

"Get up," Mr. Nightmare commanded. Neither of us turned around. There was no reason to. I wrapped my hand around Merrie's shoulder and helped her to her feet. She coughed a few times, spat in the dirt, then stood up straight.

"I'm okay," she said. I looked her in the eye and could tell it was true.

"Walk that way, my little bitches," Mr. Nightmare said. I could tell his voice was different here. I wasn't sure if Merrie could hear it, but to me it was clear. It only solidified what I was already certain of—John and Mr. Nightmare were different in the Nightmare Realm than they were in our world.

We walked down the hall at a slow but steady pace. I caught Merrie looking over at me a few times and I knew she was trying to catch my eye, maybe ask me something with a look, but I couldn't figure out what she was trying to tell me. The light came again—as before—almost out of nowhere. It was dull and red and as we kept walking it got brighter until we looked out on the Nightmare Realm. The place was the same, yet also very different, from when I'd been there earlier. The red sky persisted, but it was a deeper, darker shade of red—almost maroon. It wasn't as easy to see in the low light, but it wasn't totally dark. I looked out over the field but could only see about a quarter of what I'd seen before. The tree cage Jenn was in was barely visible, and beyond it was what appeared to be a small copse of dead trees. I couldn't see much else, though. The tree-cage I'd been trapped in was gone. Also missing was Marcus, John, and the nightmare-wolves. I wasn't upset to see those evil animals were gone.

"Jesus," Merrie whispered next to me as she scanned the place.

We took a few more tentative steps forward. Merrie kept

looking around, but my eyes were locked on Jenn's tree-cage. I gave a quick check behind me to see if Mr. Nightmare was still there and he was, a few steps back, guiding us into his world but letting us look around and see what he wanted us to see. As I got closer to the cage, I could tell there was a shadowy form inside. Jenn was either sleeping, or maybe passed out from fear or lack of food or water.

"Jenn," I said, watching for any movement inside the cage, but there was none. "What did you do to her?"

"Nothing at all, Anna," Mr. Nightmare said. "She's actually very safe. Having nightmares of course, but she will wake up unaware that any time has passed since you left. Sort of a way to keep her occupied so she wasn't screaming and yelling while you were gone."

"Where is Marcus?" Merrie asked.

The only answer to her question was silence. I kept walking toward Jenn's cage so I could get a better look and make sure she was okay. As I got closer the group of dead trees came into view. There was something there. Below the sharp points of the dead branches at the top of the group of trees, there was a mass. I couldn't tell what it was, but it was definitely not part of the trees. My stomach dropped. Merrie, still taking in the totality of the Nightmare Realm, hadn't looked at the dead trees yet. I stepped closer, let my eyes adjust to the shadows, and let the mass get clearer. It was difficult to determine what—who—was hanging up there at the center of the dead trees.

"What did you do?" I said, mostly under my breath, though loud enough for Mr. Nightmare to hear.

"A little something we rigged up for our friend Marcus," Mr. Nightmare said. I gave a quick look inside Jenn's cage, but couldn't see her, then I walked past toward the trees and to Marcus instead. Merrie must have seen me pick up my pace and change direction because she yelled out and ran toward me.

"What did you do to him?" Merrie shouted. She jogged up next to me and together we walked to the base of the tree.

Marcus was strung up, spread-eagle with his arms and legs stretched out to each side. I couldn't tell what he was tied up with at first, then realized it was thin branches or vines wrapped around his wrists and ankles. The vines were so tight they were digging into his skin and there was blood dripping down his arms and off his feet onto the tree trunk below him. His shirt was off. There were sets of long gashes across his chest, skin pulled apart revealing pink meat beneath. Blood dripped from each of the gashes and left thin rivers of blood down his chest and stomach. In spite of the blood, gore, and violence carved into Marcus's chest, it was not the cuts that caused Merrie and I to scream. Instead, it was his face. His mouth was open wide—wider than what I would consider normal, locked in a silent scream of terror. His eyes were just as terrifying to behold. They were wide open, but his pupils were gone; they had become a milky white shade. The only word I could use to describe the expression on his face was terror, pure terror. His head was tilted back looking up into the sky, like whatever was frightening him so much was up there, but invisible to me.

"Marcus!" Merrie reached up to grab his foot, which was level with our eyes.

"I wouldn't touch him," John's voice boomed from somewhere behind Mr. Nightmare. Merrie jerked her hand away and we turned. We couldn't see John right away. His shadow appeared from behind Mr. Nightmare who stood there, tall and silent, no doubt enjoying watching our anguish and fear. John stepped around the elder nightmare-eater and drew closer. Behind him, the nightmare-wolves padded along, keeping a few feet distant from their master. John stopped a few feet in front of us, the wolves halted two or three steps behind him and sat.

"What the fuck did you do to him?" Merrie said. Her muscles tensed and her fist closed tight around the knife still hidden in her hand. We'd have a hell of a time with those nightmare-wolves, but we had both of them together. The time to use the knives was approaching fast.

"Remember the day at the Dwelling, when I jumped inside Mr. Nightmare?" John's voice was calmer, more like himself, more like the voice I remembered. Neither Merrie nor I said anything so he continued. "I jumped inside him because it was *your* idea, Anna. The pain that I felt collecting those dreams, the fear, the discomfort I felt, now it's Marcus's turn to feel it. What he has been experiencing since he got here, I experienced in a few seconds. You think it was bad when Chuckie died? You have no idea the horrors that people dream at night. And I was just a kid. I had to see all those nightmares all at once. You don't know what it does to a person. But, Marcus knows. Now he knows."

The three of us looked up at Marcus. His face moved slightly, but he was still locked in terror, living through whatever he was seeing or feeling. John continued, "He can't see you or hear you right now. He doesn't even know where he is. The only thing he knows is the non-stop nightmares he's experiencing. Hours and hours of them, as far as he knows. His own worst nightmares running non-stop inside his head."

Merrie took a step toward John but I reached out and grabbed her arm. We needed to attack together at the same time. She knew that and nodded. Even in our anger we needed to maintain composure to get what we wanted.

"Why would you do that to him?" Merrie said. "He came here because he was your friend, John. He wanted to end this without anyone getting hurt, just let everyone move on with their lives."

"Like my life?" John said. "I'm stuck here because of you. Mostly because of her." He pointed at me. "But you all played a part in it, and now I'm going to make sure you all stay here with me."

"What do you mean, stay here with you?" I said. Merrie and I inched forward. The nightmare-wolves behind John stirred.

Even if he and Mr. Nightmare didn't realize we were closing the distance, those dogs did. They knew something was up. I still hoped for the element of surprise.

"He's about halfway through the process now," Mr. Nightmare spoke up. "When he's done, he will be one of us. A nightmare-eater, if you will. Then we will tie you up there, Merrie. And finally, Anna-banana. After that we will let your friend leave. She will have nightmares of this place for years to come and will be able to feed one of us for quite some time."

"You son of a bitch," Merrie spat through her teeth at them, then turned and looked at me. "Now."

The single word was all it took. I was ready. This was our only chance. They thought Merrie was out of control and emotional—and maybe she was—but she'd used it to get us close enough to them for a desperate lunge. Our odds weren't great, but we didn't know if we'd get another chance. Our prospects were bleak, anyway. We both understood, but attacked anyway. When Merrie gave the word, we both took our shot.

Merrie took two hard steps toward John and flipped the knife around like someone who'd been training for this kind of thing her entire life. I didn't have much time to see the result because I went for Mr. Nightmare at the same time, only a half-step behind Merrie. I twisted the blade out in front of me and aimed for any part of Mr. Nightmare's body I could reach. He reacted faster than I thought, but he didn't step back away from me as I'd expected. Instead, he threw his hands up like a boxer blocking a punch. But I wasn't trying to hit him with a fist, and the blade of the knife swiped hard along his forearm. Mr. Nightmare flinched back and screamed in pain. I'd done it. I'd hurt him. He turned away from me for a moment and clutched at his arm in obvious pain. In the background, there was the snarling and barking of nightmare-wolves, but I couldn't focus on them; all my attention was on my adversary. I sprinted at him, feeling no fear, only anger and the fight to survive. This was our chance. I wasn't going to fuck it up.

I charged at him while he turned toward me again. As his body spun, he brushed the hat off his head. I'd had the element of surprise, but with his hat off, Mr. Nightmare had the advantage. Even in the low light, all I had to do was look up and I'd see his face. My only chance was to keep my eyes down. I had to, or the fight would be over before it started.

As the hat drifted to the ground and I averted my eyes, I caught a glimpse of the side of his face. Everything spun and for a moment I lost my center of gravity. It felt like I was going to crash down to the ground hard. I managed to get my eyes away and focused on the center of his body instead of his face, like I'd learned in basketball. If you focus on the center of a person's body, they can't get you off balance. The dizziness was gone as soon as my gaze moved. I watched the center of his body and resumed my charge. Mr. Nightmare lashed out at me with a fist, but I was able to duck out of the way and plunge the knife into his midsection. Unlike the last time I tried to stab Mr. Nightmare, as a kid, the knife slid right in and stopped. He clutched his stomach and his knees buckled; his face was almost even with mine. I had to look away as I felt the world begin to spin a second time.

"Anna!" Merrie shouted, as I stood over Mr. Nightmare, certain I'd killed him. I turned and saw John on one knee looking at an apparent cut on his thigh. Past him, Merrie was also on her knees, holding the knife out in front of her, surrounded by the pack of snarling nightmare-wolves.

I took two steps toward her and a tree shot up from the ground in front of me. The trunk grew high into the blood-red sky above. I attempted to turn and make a run for it, but a second tree exploded from the ground to join the first, growing in a matter of seconds. Dead branches appeared around all sides of me, but instead of forming a cage around me, they twisted themselves around my legs first, then my arms, and pulled me up off the ground, lifting me into the air with them.

"Anna!" Merrie shouted a second time, this time looking up at me. The nightmare-wolves had stopped closing in on her and John had regained his feet. He'd taken his hat off as well but I was lucky enough to be unable to see his face. I could hear both him and Mr. Nightmare though. They were laughing.

CHAPTER 33

There was no way to tell how long I was suspended up above the Nightmare Realm. The air was thin up there and it was difficult to breath. I attempted to keep an eye on what was happening below, but the trees and branches around me grew in such a way that I had to crane my neck back over my left shoulder to even get a glimpse of the ground. For a while, I tried to keep looking back every so often to make sure Merrie, Jenn and Marcus were all right. But each time I did, a sharp shooting pain worked its way from my lower back all the way up to the base of my skull. In the end, I stared up at the sky and prayed nothing would happen to any of my friends.

It was quiet down there. Every once in a while there was the yelp or whine of one of the nightmare-wolves. Sometimes I could hear John's or Mr. Nightmare's voice, but I couldn't make out what they were saying. I heard nothing from Merrie, Marcus, or Jenn. They were either talking too quietly for me to hear or, more likely, not talking at all.

Sleep was something I neither wanted nor could attain while being suspended by my arms and legs—although there may have been a branch against my back or my ass helping to keep me up. Instead, I watched the sky. I tried to imagine what life was like in a place like this. Above, the sky was not starless as I'd originally thought. I could make out small pin-pricks of white light on the otherwise maroon canvas. They were tiny, nearly invisible to my eyes; if I focused on one section of the sky, I could see them. A few bird-like creatures flew past. They looked like birds—large ones—but, judging by everything else there, I assumed they were not birds in the same way I thought of them. I waited and watched, wondering when I was going to be filled in on exactly what my role was in all of this. John and Mr. Nightmare obviously had a plan for what they wanted to do with us—with the Nightmare Club. All of us were there—all except Chuck—and they must have been putting their plan into action. But up there, blind and unaware of events unfolding below me, I could only guess. We'd hurt—but not killed—the two of them. They should have retaliated; Mr. Nightmare should have called Merrie a little bitch or shoved his face into mine and forced me to pass out, but none of that happened. They were hurt, but they didn't seem angry. Satisfied, it seemed, to move forward with their plan instead. Not knowing what was next made the waiting even harder.

"Hello up there." John's voice boomed over the unending silence.

"What do you want?" I shouted, turning my head for only a second before the cramp began again in the small of my back.

John and Mr. Nightmare both laughed.

"We've finished with your friends," Mr. Nightmare said.

"It's your turn now, Anna-banana." As soon as John finished saying the words, the trees began to shrink. They still held me tight, but I descended back to the ground, cradled tightly by the branches that had held me safely in the air for so long. The trees laid me gently on the ground and continued shrinking away until I was left there, curled up in the dirt with nothing around me. My back and neck spasmed once more as tight muscles relaxed on flat earth.

I got to my feet as fast as possible. John and Mr. Nightmare had their hats on again and seemed uninjured; our attack had no long-term impact on them from what I could see. Marcus was still there, suspended above the ground, still locked in a perpetual nightmare scream. His eyes were wide and white with fear. It was hard to look at him for too long. There was no sign of Merrie and it had gotten darker, so I could no longer see Jenn's tree cage. I hoped she was still inside. But I also doubted it was true.

"Where are the others?" I walked up to John, my chest out, back straight, I almost looked him in the eye—almost. The pack of Nightmare-wolves lay on the ground behind John, and when I approached, two of them got up and let out a low growl. They took a step toward me but John waved his hand at them. They looked up at him for a second. One tilted its head to the side, looked at John, then at me, then both returned to the ground, flat on their stomachs, heads on their paws.

"This way." John put a hand on my shoulder. I thought he was going to shove me or push me to the ground, but he didn't. Instead, he guided me as we turned around. Mr. Nightmare and the nightmare-wolves fell in behind us as we walked shoulder to shoulder. I was reminded of one of the times we walked down Redbird Lane as kids. It was dark—like it was in the Nightmare Realm— I believe Merrie was on the other side of John, the three of us locked arm in arm. We were on our way to tell scary stories. Chuck was still alive and everything was good. There was no Mr. Nightmare, yet. We had no worries. Maybe my crush on John had already started developing then, I couldn't be certain. Most of the time I didn't think of him as my crush, I only thought of him as my friend. Those were great days. Now things were completely different. I didn't want John to touch me. I didn't want to feel his arm interlocked with mine. It had only been ten years.

"You're awful quiet now, huh?" John said. His voice was different, almost kid-like. Something was up. I couldn't let him string me up in one of those trees like he'd done to Marcus. If the other girls were already strung up too, I was everyone's last hope. I needed to be on guard, to be ready and fight if that happened. If I allowed them to take me too, then we'd all be stuck in the Nightmare Realm forever.

"Why are you doing this, John? What would your parents think if they knew you were doing this? Or Chuck?" I was running out of options and hoped I could make him realize he wasn't the same person I knew anymore. I wanted to remind him once more about our past. Instead, without warning, his hand flew up toward my face. I didn't have time to react and the back of his hand connected with my cheek. My head snapped to the side; I stumbled to my left but didn't fall over. The nightmare-wolves took a few steps back and to the side, giving me room.

"That was a mistake," Mr. Nightmare said. Then he laughed.

"Don't talk about them," John said. "I only see them when they're sleeping because of you. They can't know I'm still here. And don't talk about Chuck either. You don't know what the fuck he thought all the time. We weren't blood, but he was my brother too, you know."

"Fuck you, John." I almost stared into his eyes again when I said it. "I don't know everything he thought, but I know he wouldn't want this. So whatever else you have to do, go ahead and do it. He wouldn't want you to do this to me and you *know* that. Even if Mr. Nightmare has been filling your mind with terrible things about me and Merrie and Marcus for the last ten years, if you really sit back and remember the way things happened, you know that. Maybe you can't see it anymore but it's true. Regardless, Chuck would never want you doing this to us—to me. So, whatever you're going to do, kill me or make me have nightmares, I *know* he wouldn't want that. So go on thinking whatever you want. I'm done trying to convince you of something I know is true."

I looked into his chest and didn't look away. I wasn't going to back down from him on my own. If he wanted me to back down, he was going to have to make me.

"Don't fall for her tricks, John." Mr. Nightmare's voice was quiet. He slid forward until he was right next to his protégé.

"I'm not," John said, and he turned to me. "Come one, let's see your friends."

We walked another half minute. There were more twisted, dead trees on the horizon. I knew what I was going to see, but I still walked toward them, refusing avert my eyes. John and Mr. Nightmare wanted to see me flinch and look away or collapse down to the ground and scream. I wasn't going to do any of those things.

In a tangle of three dead trees to my left, was Merrie. She had thin branches wrapped around her wrists holding her arms out to either side. Her legs were spread to either side as well. Her shirt was soaked in blood. Her face was like Marcus's had been, locked in a scream, though no sound was coming out. Her eyes were wide and white. My body trembled. If I made a move toward her, they would have stopped me and probably put me up in a tree of my own, so I remained still. Jenn was strung up in a similar manner, her dirty blonde hair hung over half of her face so I could only see one eye, but her single eye was as white and as horrifying as all the rest.

"So, what then?" I said, keeping my voice as steady and apathetic as I could. "You could have done this to me when you did this to them. You had me up in that tree. Why make me stand here and look at it? Like I said before, do what you're going to do, John. Remember your parents and Chuck *wouldn't want this*." I said it loud and slow with my teeth grinding together. I knew it would piss him off and I was ready for the repercussions.

John's hand came toward my face again, fast; I didn't have time to flinch. But it stopped before he could make contact with me. Mr. Nightmare was there. He caught John's arm. For the first time ever, I saw the milky white skin of Mr. Nightmare's hand. His fingers were long and thin—like the rest of his body —his knuckles, large boney knobs.

"She wants you to hit her again." Mr. Nightmare's voice was hard and intense. "She's right. Either you do this or you don't. Stop fucking around and do it."

The two living nightmares looked at each other, hats shrouding their faces. For a long moment neither of them moved, neither did I. I thought maybe my words had changed something. Maybe John realized I was right. He understood what I'd been saying this whole time. He could send the pack of nightmare-wolves at Mr. Nightmare. They could surround him and keep him at bay while John released my friends and helped us all escape. Even after everything that happened, I still held out hope. I watched John for a sign his mind had changed. Instead, he looked at Mr. Nightmare and nodded.

An earthquake rocked the Nightmare Realm. I jumped forward as I realized it wasn't an earthquake but three massive tree trunks shooting out of the dry soil. The trunks surged past me. Dead branches grabbed and pulled at me. They wrapped first around my wrists and then my ankles, pulling me in four directions at once. White hot pain burned my chest and I looked down as blooms of red soaked and spread through the fabric of my shirt. John and Mr. Nightmare spoke below me but I couldn't understand their words. I opened my mouth to scream but nothing came out.

Then came the nightmares.

CHAPTER 34

I knew I was asleep. I *knew* I was dreaming, but there was nothing I could do to stop it. Nothing I could do to end it. The moment my eyes closed I expected everything to go dark. It did not. Instead, I saw only white. White, like the eyes of my friends. I was like them: my mouth open wide in a silent scream and my eyes milky white, held aloft by a dead tree, dripping blood on the ground far below.

Knowing what my body looked like out there in the Nightmare Realm was not what scared me the most. In a single, fleeting moment, as the world went white around me, I wasn't scared of the fact that I was doomed to spend the rest of my life in the Nightmare Realm eating nightmares with the others. I didn't fear the fact my mom and dad would have lost a second child for reasons they would never really understand. I was sad for them, but I didn't fear it. Only one thing scared me, the only true fear I felt was knowing the nightmares were coming and there was nothing I could do to stop them.

The bleached, blank world slowly faded, and I found myself walking through someone's back yard. At first, the lush green grass reminded me of the Field we'd played at when we were kids. As everything came into focus, however, I could see the back of a house in front of me and a street beyond. I didn't recognize the house or the street so I kept walking forward. My feet felt as though they weren't moving, but I continued anyway.

"It's because you're dreaming, Anna," I said, realizing what was happening. "Just keep going."

And I did. I went through the backyard and looked at the house from the front, but still didn't recognize it. I got to the street and looked both ways. There was no traffic, but I'd always done it, so I looked left then right and planned to turn and follow the street until I figured out where I was. Nothing looked familiar and every house on the street looked exactly the same. The road stretched as far as I could see in both directions. The same white house with black shutters lined both sides with about ten feet separating each house. I wanted to turn left, but instead, I kept walking across the street. I had no idea where I was headed, but I couldn't end my dream, so I didn't try to fight it, letting the dream play out.

When I crossed the street, I slipped in between two identical houses and found myself in a back yard. I didn't walk because my feet still weren't moving. I looked up. I was behind the same house I'd been behind before. The yard was the same, everything was the same as when I first entered the dream. I kept going and passed through the same back yard six times. Nothing changed. I wondered if this entire thing *was* the nightmare. An unending repetition that didn't change no matter how much I wanted it to. It seemed like the kind of sick twisted hell Mr. Nightmare would dream up for me. I continued on— because I had no choice—until I heard a voice call out from up ahead.

"Hey, man," the voice said, and there was knocking like someone pounding on a door. "You home?"

I couldn't see who it was but something about the voice was familiar. It sounded like a young kid. I kept going.

"Hello?" I called out, but there was no response.

I wanted to move faster. I wanted to see who was there with me. Was it someone else caught in a weird nightmare tree like I was? Or maybe it was one of the others I'd seen with Mr. Nightmare when I first entered the Nightmare Realm. I wanted to move faster—to run—but it wasn't allowed. I continued my steady pace forward.

"Hello?" I called out again. Still no answer.

I got to the side of the house and looked out across the street. The opposite side was still lined with identical houses.

All but one house.

I recognized it immediately and understood what John and Mr. Nightmare had in mind for me. It was the worst thing I could imagine. The different house was the one Marcus lived in when we were kids. And the person I'd heard talking was Chuck. He sat on the front step of Marcus's childhood home looking across the street. Looking right at me.

"Chuck!" I shouted. I wanted to run to him but was held in place, unable to move forward. I knew I was dreaming and knew Mr. Nightmare or John were controlling what I saw, but those thoughts slipped away when I saw Chuck. Part of me didn't expect him to hear or see me when I called to him, but he did hear me. He stood up when I called his name and looked over at me.

"Anna?" he said. "I thought you were staying at the Field while I came to get Marcus. What are you doing here?"

He got up and made his way down the front walk of Marcus's house toward me. I knew everything that was going to take place but was unable to stop it.

I looked both ways again, not for my sake, I still wasn't allowed to move, but for Chuck. I knew what was coming and wanted to stop it.

"Chuck," I shouted. "No, stay there," I said, but he didn't stop, and he didn't look both ways as he approached the street. It wouldn't have mattered. When he stepped off the grass and onto the pavement, I heard it. The loud roar of an engine. It was there. It had appeared out of nowhere and was only a few feet from Chuck, barreling down on him fast. The windows of the car were dark, tinted, but I could see the silhouette of a man in a top hat behind the wheel.

"Chuck, look out!" I shouted again, hoping he'd react in time to dive out of the way. He didn't even turn his head. He didn't even see the car as it came at him.

He continued on, walking out into the road.

I screamed.

The front of the car smashed into Chuck's body. It was like watching in slow motion. His body made contact with the front grill and dented it inward. Chuck's eyes got wide as the force of the car pinned his arm against him and bent his body into a sideways 'V.' His head slammed off the hood of the car, and I could hear his skull crack as it made contact. His feet and legs disappeared underneath the car at nearly the same moment. Then he was flying through the air, the impact sending him at least ten feet backwards. He landed with a thud on the pavement, rolled once, and didn't move again. His eyes were still open though. He was still looking at me. But his life had ended.

I shook. Every part of my body wanted to run to him, to help him. To call the ambulance. The first time he'd been on the ground for a few minutes before anyone noticed. Maybe a fast call to 9-1-1 could save his life. I wanted to rush to him but I was held in place, watching from across the street.

"No, please, Chuck, no!" I shouted. Tears rolled down my face. I screamed and stared at his lifeless body. My stomach churned and I collapsed to the ground. I vomited into the green grass, then curled up in a ball and cried. If there was one saving grace in Chuck's death out there in the real world, it was that I never had to see him get hit by that car. I never had to watch him die. Now, I'd seen it.

I don't know how long I was there, lying in the grass, but at some point I got up. I was standing once again in someone's back yard. I knew I was still dreaming. I remembered the dream of seeing Chuck get hit by the car—get hit by Mr. Nightmare—but like most dreams, even as I thought about it, it started to fade.

I walked through the back yard and looked across at a row of houses. They were all the same except for one. Chuck sat on the front step of the house and looked up at me when I came into view.

"Anna?" he said as he got up and started to walk toward me. "What are you doing here?"

I screamed.

CHAPTER 35

I don't know how many times they forced me to watch the same thing because it never stopped. Each time Chuck died, his lifeless eyes stared back at me as if blaming me for not being there when it happened, or blaming me for being the reason he crossed the street in the first place. It was possible he wished I'd been there at the end. It didn't matter if it was real or not. Each time I watched Chuck get hit by the car and each time I watched him die, it was as excruciating to see as the first time. It never got easier.

Watching Chuck die over and over was the worst part, but almost as bad was that for a split second, as the whole scene reset in my head, I remembered I was dreaming and I'd been strung up and forced to see my nightmare over and over again. For a second, I knew what I was going to see, what I'd just seen, and what was happening outside of this dream world. What I didn't know was how long I'd been trapped in my nightmare and how long I was going to stay there. What if I'd already seen Chuck die a thousand times? And what if I'd only been dreaming a few minutes? By the end of it all I could watch him die a billion times—maybe more. There was no way to tell.

I watched Chuck die again. I screamed again and the entire

world began to reset around me. I was in that sliver of space when I knew what was happening to me and understood it all. I knew what to expect next. The scene was about to replay for me once more. Instead, something changed. At first, I was aware of it, but couldn't react.

"Anna," a voice said. I heard it, but it didn't register right away. It wasn't Chuck's voice and it felt like part of the dream.

I was sitting in the backyard of the random house, about to walk into the front yard and see my brother get hit by a car yet again, when the voice called out to me once more.

"Anna, wake the fuck up. Hurry," the voice said. It didn't belong there. In a subconscious part of my mind, I knew it wasn't how the dream was supposed to go. The voice still sounded familiar, but I couldn't place it. I was lost between the dream world and the real one and couldn't comprehend what was happening.

"Who is it?" I managed to say. I didn't know if I said it aloud or inside my dream world. I still couldn't tell the difference. Then the voice responded to my question.

"Anna, it's Marcus. Get the fuck up and hurry," he said.

Marcus? He was in his house. Chuck was waiting for him. The voice talking to me didn't sound like the kid Marcus, though. It sounded like adult Marcus. Adult Marcus. Yes. My head cleared all at once. The dream world faded and I blinked. The red sky overhead told me I was back in the Nightmare Realm. I blinked again. My head throbbed and I moved to grab at it, but my arms were pinned on either side of me. Everything came rushing back at once. I knew where I was and why I was there.

"Marcus," I said, my voice only a whisper. He was in the tree with me somehow. I could feel him pulling at the branches holding my arms in place.

"Welcome back. We have to get the three of you out of here," he said. He pulled hard and one of my hands fell free, then he went to work on the other one. "They were more out of it than you were. It took me forever to wake them up. You don't have a lot of time."

"What do you mean?" I said. "You're coming back too?"

He kept working on my other hand and didn't say anything. When he was done and my other arm was free, he effortlessly moved himself down to my ankles while I wrapped my hands around the remaining branches so I wouldn't fall off. Marcus let one of my legs loose then the other, then grabbed my waist and lowered me down to the ground. He laid me gently on the dirt. I looked up and saw Jenn and Merrie sitting on the ground looking at me. Merrie's eyes were red, her cheeks puffy. Jenn didn't look good either, but she didn't look as bad as Merrie. My entire body ached, but I scrambled to my feet anyway.

"Come on," I said. "Let's get out of here. We can all make it, Marcus, you don't have to stay to hold them off."

As I stood up, I realized something was wrong. Merrie stood up, then Jenn. The four of us stood there but Marcus was taller than us. A lot taller. Merrie looked at him but he kept his head turned away. He'd become one of them now. Whatever John and Mr. Nightmare had done to him, they'd done enough to change him. He was a nightmare-eater. It hadn't changed him mentally yet, but the physical change was clear.

"Shit," I said under my breath. I understood why Merrie had been crying. And she stared at me because she knew I understood exactly what she was going though. I might have been younger when I lost John to this place, but the feelings didn't change.

"I don't understand it, but John didn't change right away either," Marcus said. I nodded. He was right, the change in John took place over years. Marcus could still help us, but it meant saying goodbye quickly and not knowing what would happen to him if he let us leave.

"Where are they?" Jenn said. Her voice was gravelly as if she'd been screaming for hours. She probably had been.

"I don't know," Marcus said. "But you need to go. To be

honest, I'd rather them kill me than stay like this, so let's get you out of here and I'll face whatever punishment they have for me, but we've got to get you three out now."

Jenn and I agreed, and were ready to follow Marcus across to the yawning mouth of the cave. Merrie didn't move.

"I can't," she said. Her eyes were sad but her voice was flat; there was no emotion there. I knew how she felt and I went to her, but Marcus stopped me with a hand on my shoulder. I turned to him and he turned away, not giving me the chance to see his face.

"I got this," Marcus said. He took a few smooth strides to Merrie. I hung back. Jenn put her arm around my waist, my arm went around her shoulder, and I pulled her against me. I hadn't talked to her since we'd been in the tree cages. We kept our distance, giving Merrie and Marcus the time they needed. I couldn't hear what Marcus was saying but he was animated, probably due to the time constraints we were under, and Merrie was emotional.

"You doing okay?" I said to Jenn.

She sighed. "As good as can be expected. Anna, if she doesn't come along soon..." She trailed off. I'd been thinking the same thing. Merrie was my friend, but if her decision was to stay, we still needed to get out of there. Of course, I'd try to talk her out of staying, but if she wouldn't listen, then we'd have to leave without her.

"I know," I said quietly. We waited maybe another minute. The talking between Merrie and Marcus seemed to have stopped and they were standing there, shoulders touching but not looking at each other. Merrie was not only sad, she was angry too. Whether it was anger toward Marcus or John and Mr. Nightmare, I couldn't tell.

"Merrie," I said, louder so she could hear me. She took a big breath in and let it out then came over to us, Marcus was a few steps behind her.

"Come on," Marcus said when they got to us. Merrie slowed

her walk and put an arm around my shoulders while Marcus walked ahead of us, leading the way to the cave.

We were three across: I was in the middle, Merrie on my left and Jenn on my right. Marcus led us across the Nightmare Realm. There was no sign of Mr. Nightmare or John. We moved fast, and our pace quickened as we got closer to the opening. I didn't know how we would get back to our world without John or Mr. Nightmare to use as a portal, but then I realized Marcus was going to be our doorway between the worlds.

Marcus got to the opening of the cave first. He checked inside, and when there was no sign of either John or Mr. Nightmare, he waved us over.

"Come on," Marcus said, and he ushered us past him into the cave. From behind came the snarling of dogs.

We all stopped, though none of us wanted to turn around. Marcus, closest to the opening of the cave, turned, getting between us and the nightmare-wolves.

"Marcus, you're taller," John said. "I didn't think you'd be out already, but it looks like you fed off those nightmares faster than I thought you would. How does it feel to be full of all that fear?"

The nightmare-wolves spread out on either side of John and inched forward so they were in front of him. Their heads were down, like before; it told me they were ready to attack. They weren't there to scare us this time. Their black eyes glowed in the low light of the cave. Seeing one set of those eyes staring back at you would be scary enough, seeing at least twenty sets made my stomach clench in on itself. I wanted to be home.

"You're not going to let them go, right?" Marcus marched toward John, but he slowed his pace. It was strange to see them together; their long slender bodies didn't fit the kids I knew growing up.

"I wanted the Nightmare Club back together. That's it. Now it's you and me, buddy. We can get Merrie and Anna to join us and we'll be back together, like old times. Right?" John said. Mr.

Nightmare still hadn't made an appearance and I didn't know where he might be lurking. I kept an eye behind us, knowing he'd likely appear somewhere in the darkness.

"I'm not gonna let you take them." Marcus's voice was strong.

"How are you going to stop me, Marcus?" John waved his hand and a wall of dead trees burst up through the floor of the cave about two feet behind us. We were trapped, John and the wolves on one side and the wall of trees on the other.

"So, we can't leave unless we get down to the end of the cave thing?" Merrie smirked. It was good to have her back. "Thanks for the info, Johnny boy."

Marcus waved his hand at the trees, they wobbled back and forth like a strong wind had blown through the cave, but they didn't drop back down into the dirt.

John laughed. "Haven't quite figured that out yet, huh?"

Marcus waved his hand a second time and the trees dropped. Not all of them and not all the way, but they dropped enough to give us a path through the miniature forest.

"Go," Marcus said as soon as the trees dropped. I didn't know how much time we had, and turned to run, Merrie and Jenn did the same. John said something in a language I didn't understand as we took our first few steps, and the nightmare-wolves came for us. The cave filled with the echoes of snarls and barks. They weren't trying to herd us, this time they were trying to kill us. The three of us stopped for a second, but Marcus shouted again at us above the sounds of the angry wolves, telling us to keep going. We listened to him and pushed our way through the half-broken wall.

We made it about halfway through when the trees returned, more this time then when John first created the wall. Marcus ran at John, his arms wide, trying to grab at him. The wolves weren't paying any attention to Marcus—probably because he was a nightmare-eater too—they were coming for us instead.

"The trees are back," I said, since I was in front. "We need weapons. Grab a branch!"

I ripped a branch off a dead tree, surprised it actually came off in my hand, and handed it back to Merrie, who was closest to the rushing nightmare-wolves. A crack echoed as Jenn ripped off a branch of her own; I tore another free for myself a moment later. It wasn't much, but it was all we had.

When I returned my attention to the oncoming wolves, the first had already reached Merrie. She was never the best softball player but I couldn't tell from her swing. She held the branch with two hands and as the wolf lunged at her she swung hard, connecting with the side of the beast's face. The thing yelped and fell over on its side. It went down and cowered away from Merrie when it got back to its feet.

"Come on," Merrie shouted, waiting for the next wolf to come at her. "I don't think these pups like getting hit." It came at her, but this time she had Jenn on one side of her and me on the other. We were ready for the attack. I connected with a snapping wolf, but didn't make clean contact. It stumbled and came at me again as two more came up behind it. I couldn't hold all three of them off and I made a wild, arching swing hoping to clear them out and make contact with all three at once. I hit the first one clean and made a glancing blow on the backside of the second. The third nightmare-wolf was too close to me and I couldn't get my branch up fast enough to hit it. Instead of swinging I poked at it, using the branch like a spear. I hit it on the underside where its belly should have been. The branch wasn't sharp enough to break the skin, but I pushed the wolf away. While I was focused on that one, a fourth jumped over it and came at me before I had the chance to react. The only thing I had time to do was throw my arm up to protect my face from its snapping jaws.

Using my arm to keep the wolf from biting my face worked, but it clamped down around my forearm instead. I screamed and thrashed around as the teeth of the nightmare-wolf dug into the flesh of my bare arm. Luckily, the long lower fangs missed my skin. Blood seeped out around its teeth and dripped down my arm. I couldn't shake the thing off and it began twisting back and forth like a dog with a toy, tearing my flesh apart more with each twist of its body. I screamed again. I needed help but the other two girls were still fighting off other angry wolves. Another wolf came at me, looking to bite into my face or my neck instead of just my arm. I blocked out the pain and composed myself enough to give a half-hearted swipe at the thing with my branch. It wasn't hard, but it slowed the wolf down.

I pulled myself back toward the tree behind me and the wolf, still attached to my arm, pulled me in the other direction in a twisted game of tug of war. I screamed again and lifted the branch up above my head then slammed it down on the thing's head as hard as I could. It didn't let go, but I felt its grip loosen after I made contact. There were less wolves attacking us now and I realized that in spite of my current situation, we were making a difference. I grunted and heaved the branch up a second time. It slammed once more into the wolf's head. The grip loosened even more, but I could still feel its teeth cutting into my flesh. If I tried to twist away, I'd do more harm than good. I readied myself to give it another shot with the branch when something hit me from the side. Before I could even comprehend what had happened, I was on the ground. The wolf that had been on my arm fell away but there was another wolf on top of me. I shoved my uninjured forearm into its throat and pushed it back. There was just enough distance between the two of us that I could keep its snapping jaws away from my face. It worked back and forth, trying to break down my guard, but it couldn't. Drool dripped from its mouth onto my face. I could feel the beast's hot breath with each snap of its jaws. An odor of raw meat and death filled my nose. I raised my feet and kicked at its belly. When I did, there were a few soft yelps and then it went back to snapping at my face. I couldn't move and couldn't force the thing off of me. I was stuck.

Out of nowhere, a crack exploded in the cave, and immediately the wolf crumpled down on top of me. Its wet snout pressed against my face, but it had stopped moving.

"Got him for ya," Jenn said, holding half of her branch in her hand. The other half lay on the other side of the unconscious wolf. She'd broken it over the thing's head. The wolves were still moving, but it seemed as though they had lost most of the fight they had in them when they first attacked us. We'd held them off, though my arm was pretty torn up. Merrie's leg was dripping blood into her socks. We were sweating and bleeding and hadn't come out of the attack unscathed, but we'd survived.

"Where did they go?" I asked, pointing a thumb at the opening to the cave where Marcus and John had been fighting when the wolves attacked.

"No idea," Merrie said. She looked at the stirring wolves. I knew we were both thinking the same thing; we didn't have much time. "We need to move."

"Yeah, but where do we go?" Jenn sucked in heavy breaths as she spoke.

"We can't leave without using one of them as a portal," I said. "We need John or Marcus or…"

"Hello there, Anna-banana." The wall of trees disappeared and Mr. Nightmare stood, menacing with his top hat pulled down low in the darkness.

CHAPTER 36

The three of us stood, staring at Mr. Nightmare. I retreated a few steps, giving myself some distance, and joined my friends. The nightmare-eater pushed his way through the half-destroyed wall and emerged on our side. The maroon light from outside the cave made it look as though he were glowing red in front of the dark cave stretching out behind him. The wolves stirred even more, some of them getting back to their feet, though it didn't seem they were eager for another fight with us. Once Mr. Nightmare was completely on our side, he waved his hand and the wall of trees grew back to its original size. Our escape from the Nightmare Realm was blocked once again.

"What do we do?" Jenn asked. I didn't know what to tell her.

"Miss Jenn, the bartender," Mr. Nightmare said in a voice that almost sounded happy, as if laughing at us from somewhere beneath his shadowed face. "If there is anyone who should be pissed off about the way this whole thing went down, Miss Jenn, it should be you. I never wanted you here, neither did young Jonathan. The only reason you're here is because these two dragged you into their problems, and now…"

"Bullshit," Merrie blurted out before Mr. Nightmare could

even finish his thought. The whole time he'd been talking, he'd been coming toward us, but we maintained our distance from him and inched back as he moved forward. It was good to know the open mouth of the cave was behind us. If we had to, we could make a run for it even though it was likely he could stop us.

"John brought her into this when he made me drive through her family's restaurant," Merrie continued. "If that hadn't happened, she wouldn't have been so curious and she wouldn't be here right now. You love to spin shit but I'm not gonna let you do that. You did it with John but you won't do it again, asshole."

Mr. Nightmare laughed and kept moving forward. We'd backed our way past the nightmare-wolves and most of them were behind Mr. Nightmare, half of them still laying on the ground watching us, licking their wounds.

"You gonna string us back up now?" I asked. "We fought our way out once and we'll do it again. You're not going to take us. We're going to keep fighting."

"Oh, I realize that," Mr. Nightmare said, his voice dripped with smugness. Like he knew he had us and there wasn't much we could do. If that's what he was thinking, he was right. Without Marcus to help us leave, we were at the mercy of beings with powers we didn't even know about. "Coincidentally, did you like the nightmare I thought up for you, Anna-banana? I thought it was a rather nice touch to make sure you got to see one of my fondest memories over and over and over and over. It must have been horrific for you. But it made you stronger. In fact, feeding off a dream like that might have made you almost as powerful as me. I guess we'll never know."

I looked over at Merrie because, whether he meant to or not, he gave something away. He wasn't planning on putting us back in the dead trees. Maybe the whole thing was John's idea. If Mr. Nightmare didn't want us becoming like him there were only two alternatives: either he was going to let us go—unlikely, or he was going to kill us. We needed to do something.

"So, you're *not* going to turn us into nightmare-eaters now? That *was* your plan, right? To make us like you. So, now what?" Merrie said. We were almost at the mouth of the cave. I prayed Marcus would come around the corner and distract Mr. Nightmare long enough to get us to the other side of the wall, but he didn't appear.

"But not anymore," I said. "Because he didn't realize we'd be this hard to assimilate. We're not lying down and taking it like the two of you thought we would."

There was movement behind us and John staggered into view with Marcus right behind him, as if they'd been fighting. When they looked in on us, they both stopped. I realized how we looked, me holding my arm against my chest as blood soaked my shirt and the ground, blood dripping from Merrie's leg. We were a mess, but we were still standing.

"Well, here we all are," Mr. Nightmare said. "Your original group had five members, didn't it? Now we have Miss Jenn to replace Chuck, who is sadly no longer with us."

My lips tightened. He knew how to get me going, but I couldn't let him get to me. There was too much at stake. We still needed to get out of here somehow. Letting him goad me into getting angry would do nothing.

"What do you think, Arthur?" John said, addressing Mr. Nightmare by his real name. It sounded strange. "Should we try to turn them one more time? Marcus is a fast learner and will have all this stuff mastered before long. He's already learned some of the things we can do. I bet the girls here will be fast learners, too."

"This was always your endeavor, Jonathan," Mr. Nightmare said. "I was merely here for assistance. If you want to continue and give it another try, I will help. If you want to get rid of them, I will be more than happy to help with that as well. Especially the little bitch. And if you want to let them go, well, I'd be disappointed but I'd go along with that too."

John laughed. "No. There is no way I'm letting them go. Marcus's mind will clear up before long. With the three of us at full strength, we'll be able to keep them in place. As long as the others don't know we have people from the other side here, we'll be safe. We can hold them until Marcus changes his mind."

The ground shook as he finished speaking. I assumed it was a tree cage coming up to surround the three of us—a place to put us for safe keeping until they were ready to try to transform us once more. Instead, a wall of trees burst from the ground in front of John and Marcus was running toward us.

"Come on," he said, and he ran past us toward Mr. Nightmare. We ran with Marcus as John forced the dead trees back into the ground, but Marcus was able to lift them back up again. Then he raised another cage of trees around Mr. Nightmare, and we sprinted back into the cave. Mr. Nightmare pushed the trees imprisoning him to the side as we ran by. He was able to grab hold of Merrie's leg. Marcus stopped and threw his fist into Mr. Nightmare's arm hard enough to get him to release his grip. We kept going, Marcus behind us, throwing trees and bushes up from the ground in front of John and Mr. Nightmare, then replacing them with new ones once our pursuers were able to get rid of them. It was slow going because Marcus needed to remove walls they put in front of us, as well, but we kept moving forward and made it further into the cave until the light was so dim we could barely see.

"I feel something here," Marcus said, looking back over his shoulder. "Something's different here. I think this is the place."

"Are you sure?" Jenn said.

Mr. Nightmare and John were still coming at us. Marcus did his best holding them off with the trees.

"No, but we have to try," Marcus said. "I can't slow them down forever."

"Yeah," I said. "Let's go. No hesitation." I looked at Merrie and she nodded. Marcus raised his hand and brought a final wall up, then stood still with his arms in the air.

"I love you," he said. It was to all of us, but mostly for Merrie.

"Love you, Marcus," I said "Thank you."

"I love you," Merrie said. He had his head turned away from us so we wouldn't see his face. Merrie took his chin in her hand and turned his face to hers. She looked up at him. In the dim light, I could see her eyes roll back in her head and she gagged. There wasn't time to wait for her to regain consciousness so I grabbed her hand and Jenn's hand at the same time then pulled them toward Marcus. For a second, I thought we'd run right into him and we wouldn't be able to get home, but everything went cold and black and then we were inside him. The next thing I knew, we were looking up at the night sky, laying on a pile of wood at the destroyed farmhouse.

CHAPTER 37

I blinked a few times. I expected it to be daytime, but it was dark out. Since we had no idea how long we were strapped to those trees, seeing our own nightmares, there was no telling what day it was. I was exhausted and could have laid there and fallen asleep, but we weren't safe.

"We have to get out of here," Merrie said before I could say the same thing.

"You think they'll still come after us?" Jenn said. I was confused at first then realized how much she still didn't understand about Mr. Nightmare. It felt as though she'd been part of the group all along, but she'd only known about Mr. Nightmare for a few days—although a lot had happened in those few days.

"Yeah," I said and ran toward my car, surprised to find the keys still in my pocket after all that had happened. "Let's go."

We ran up and over the broken wood, toward the Dying Buffalo, parked right where I'd left it. Our steps were hard and fast, not the slow cautious steps Merrie and I had taken when we were last there. So much had changed and with the injuries we'd already sustained, a cut on the foot or ankle was of little consequence.

We piled into my car, it roared to life, and I drove away.

There was little talking at first. Mr. Nightmare had told them what my nightmare was, but I had no idea what theirs were. Knowing he picked the most traumatic event I'd experienced in my life made me think the other girls had life changing dreams of their own to deal with. I was driving home but realized that idea wasn't going to work. We didn't know how long we'd been gone, and having to deal with questions about our where-abouts, as well as the whereabouts of Marcus, was not some-thing I thought we were ready for. We needed to regroup and figure out what we were going to tell the police if they were involved—because Jenn had been missing for a long time. And also, how we were going to deal with John and Mr. Nightmare when they inevitably came for us again. It wasn't going to end with our narrow escape. Our escape kept us alive and stopped the metamorphosis into nightmare-eaters, but it didn't end everything. They would come for us, and they had powers in our world too. The threat was still there; our escape made it more likely they would come here and kill us as soon as they could. They had no need for us anymore.

"We can't go home yet," I said. I guided the car around a turn that would lead us to Marcus's apartment instead of back to my neighborhood.

"Anna, I have to…" Jenn started, but Merrie interrupted her.

"No, she's right," Merrie said. She reached up and put a hand on Jenn's shoulder. "Listen, time is different here than it is there. You were already missing a while when Anna got back. The fact that you weren't with Anna when she popped back up is going to make people worry. We need rest and we need a cover story. If we go back to any of our houses right now there will be a million questions. Marcus lives by himself. He doesn't talk to his parents every day. We can regroup there. Figure something out to tell people or, better yet, figure out how to stop John and Mr. Nightmare for good. Trust us."

Jenn looked at me and I glanced over.

"We'll take care of you," I said. "Let's get some rest and

figure this out. Then we can all go home."

Jenn looked worried and I didn't blame her. Merrie and I were acting like we knew what the hell we were doing, but we were flying by the seat of our pants and making things up as we went. It had been a long time since we were running around the neighborhood as kids fighting an evil monster who ate our dreams. Though Jenn took our word for it because we'd been through it before, everything was a guess.

When we got to the apartment, Merrie let us in with her key. My arm had stopped bleeding as had Merrie's leg, but I let her use the only shower first. Jenn and I sat in the kitchen for a while, then she went out onto the balcony and had a cigarette while I found a couple beers in Marcus's fridge. Not wanting to be alone, I joined Jenn outside. I slid the door closed behind me and sat in the white plastic chair Marcus had out there. I tossed Jenn a beer.

"To another sunrise?" I said, looking up at the night sky.

"Let's not get too far ahead of ourselves. The sun isn't up yet," she said, then cracked open the can. I did the same.

"Well, to another night then," I said, and drank about half the can in one gulp. It was cold and felt good. I probably needed water but the beer was heaven. I looked up at stars. I recalled the stars in the blood-red night sky of the Nightmare Realm. Were those the same ones I saw sitting on Marcus's balcony? I knew more about Mr. Nightmare than I did a few weeks ago, but there was still so much I didn't know. I flexed my hand and looked at my forearm. The spots where the teeth had cut into my arm throbbed and burned. The torn flesh looked bad but not terrible. It would heal and it could have been a lot worse. I put the cold can on the wounds.

"Can I ask you a question?" I said.

"Course." Jenn took another sip of her beer.

"What was your nightmare?"

Jenn sighed but didn't answer right away. After a few minutes, I figured she didn't want to tell me.

"It's okay if you don't want to say," I said. "It's personal. I understand."

"No," Jenn said. "I mean, it *is* personal, but I was just trying to remember it all. Even though I saw it like a million times, its fuzzy at the same time, you know?"

"Yeah," I said. I did kind of understand. Even though I recalled the major details of my own dream, certain parts of it were fuzzy and less clear.

"When I was a kid," Jenn said, "my biggest fear was always that someone would break into our house while we were sleeping. They'd kill my parents and leave me because I was just a kid. Then I'd have to go live with my grandparents or something. Normal kid fears, right? Well, I had this recurring nightmare about it. From first grade all though elementary school, once a month I'd wake up screaming. When my parents asked what was wrong, I'd just tell them it was a bad dream and move on. Sometimes I'd tell them I dreamed they died. But the recurring dream was more than just that they died. It was the break-in, an incredibly violent death, and then me screaming and crying over their dead bodies until I woke up."

"Wow, and that was your dream in there?" I asked, assuming Mr. Nightmare could somehow see her dream from when she was a kid.

"Yes and no," Jenn said. "In there, up on that tree, it was the same but not the same. It started the same. I was a little kid again. I woke up in bed and heard a noise down the hall in my parents' room. When I got there, there was someone on their bed just slamming a knife down through the sheets into their bodies. But the sheets and the person— everything, was dripping with blood. I hid and watched, then the person just got off the bed and left though the bedroom window. I got on the bed and screamed until I woke up, just like in my recurring dream. But when I woke up, I was still in the dream. I was back in bed. So, I got up and went to their room again and there was someone else killing them in a different way. The person left and I ran to them again. I was stuck in a loop and had to watch my parents die in different ways over and over again. It was terrible." There was a long pause; neither of us said anything. Jenn sniffled then looked up at me, her eyes wet. "Yours was watching Chuck die?"

I nodded. Merrie slid the door open and joined us on the balcony. She had a beer in her hand too. There wasn't another chair, but I got up when I saw her limp out and let her have my seat. She opened the can and took a long sip, then leaned back and closed her eyes.

"Feel better?" I asked.

Merrie nodded. "Marcus has a good first aid box, so I was able to wrap up my leg and put some gauze on the bites. They aren't that deep and look worse than they are, I think. After you clean up, I can get you wrapped up too."

"Okay," I said. "Those wolf things should have been able to take us out, no problem. We fought back but there were so many of them. They could have killed us if they really wanted to. These bites should be worse than they are."

"I thought the same thing," Merrie said. "What does it mean, though?"

I shrugged. "Could mean anything. They aren't really the kind of nightmare-wolves who fight and kill, they just look vicious."

"Or," Jenn jumped in, "the person who controls them told them to take it easy on us."

Merrie and I shared a look.

"Yeah," Merrie said. "That too."

"Well," I said. "If he called off the dogs it's because he wanted to do something else fucked up to us. I'm done giving John the benefit of the doubt. He had a few chances with me and I was dumb for not seeing through him. I'm not going to fall for it again. When we get the chance to end this, we're ending it for both of them because they're both just as evil in my book."

There wasn't much else to say after that. We sat and drank our beers and looked up at the sky. My legs shook as I stood there, exhaustion taking hold of my body.

"I'm going to go shower," I said. "Unless you want to go first, Jenn."

"No," she said. "I'm not as bloody as you. Go clean up and then I can go last while Merrie wraps you up. Then food and sleep?"

"Yes," Merrie and I both said at the same time. I was starving but the remaining bit of adrenaline flowing through my body meant I didn't realize how hungry I was until Jenn mentioned it.

I left them out on the balcony and found my way to Marcus's bathroom. The fan was on and the room still steamy from Merrie's shower. I thought of showers at my parents' place. There, I would have had to wait a half hour for the hot water to return before I could hop in. At least in the apartment complex there was no waiting involved.

I turned on the water, peeled my clothes off and got in. I kept it cool at first; it felt good on my sweaty, sticky body. The water at my feet was pink and I watched it swirl down the drain. I rubbed the cool water on my arm until the dried blood was gone. Then I incrementally turned the hot water up, letting it warm and rinse the Nightmare Realm from my body for the second time. As the water rushed down around my head, I ran through the events of the summer. I thought about the day I met Merrie and Marcus for pizza—neither of them wanted to talk about the Nightmare Club. Then there was the first time I went to Marcus's apartment; we were convinced John was calling to us and trying to contact us. He *was* trying to contact us, but he wasn't looking for help. He was looking to have us join him. If I hadn't brought it up with them and made them remember, we might not have found ourselves in this situation. When I heard John calling, I assumed it was the wind. If I hadn't brought Merrie and Marcus into it, I'd still be assuming it was the wind.

We never would have gone to the Shaw Farm. Merrie wouldn't have crashed her car into the front window of the bar and Jenn wouldn't have been involved at all. All of this could have been avoided if *I'd* done things differently. Merrie, Marcus and Jenn were my friends—good friends—they'd do anything for me. But they shouldn't have *had* to do this for me. This was my mistake and I needed to make things right. I needed to fix this, and I needed to do it without Merrie or Jenn.

Neither of them would allow me to do it myself. I could practically hear Merrie's protest in my head. 'We're in this together,' she would say. If I was going to fix it on my own, I was going to have to be sneaky about it. And I still didn't really have an idea of *how* to fix it. Before I could deal with that, however, I had to figure out how to get out of there without them noticing.

I finished up my shower and got out. I wrapped a towel around me and went to the balcony to get Merrie. She came in with Jenn behind her. Jenn went into the bathroom, and Merrie and I want into Marcus's bedroom, where she cleaned my cuts —which were shallow, like Merrie's had been. When she was done, she got me some of Marcus's clothes to wear.

"What are we going to do, Anna?" she said, sitting on the bed while I got dressed.

"I don't know," I sighed. At least there was *some* truth in what I was saying. "Right now, we have to hope Marcus is giving them a hell of a time over there. Maybe they'll think it won't be worth it."

"Yeah," Merrie laughed. "Maybe. But I doubt it."

"Me too," I said. "We need to figure something out. If they can, they will come back for us."

"I know." Merrie got up. I could see her hands shaking; she was as hungry as I was. "Maybe we can stop them from coming here."

Merrie left the room. I followed her out, but an idea was forming.

CHAPTER 38

M arcus had some frozen chicken nuggets, so we threw them in the stove, but we couldn't wait for them to cook, so we had cereal and peanut butter sandwiches while they warmed up. We downed the peanut butter sandwiches with another round of beers, and I could feel some of the tension in my body release. We even laughed while we talked and ate. My hands were still shaking when I finished my peanut butter sandwich but luckily the nuggets were just about done. We dipped the nuggets in ketchup instead of barbecue sauce because it was all Marcus had. By the time we'd finished all of the nuggets, we were full and it was getting late. We didn't know what the next day would bring. There was no sign of Mr. Nightmare or John, and we wanted to rest while we still could.

"Listen," I said, stretching my arms up over my head. My body was sore and exhausted. Lying down was going to feel amazing, but I wasn't planning on giving myself much sleep. "I know we're all thinking the same thing here. I think Merrie should take the bed."

"Yes," Jenn agreed. "Totally take the bed. I could sleep anywhere right now."

"Well, I don't mind sharing the bed," Merrie said, exactly

what I'd hoped she would. I wanted to get both of them in the bedroom so I could make an escape once they were asleep.

"You two should take the bed then," I said. Then I continued before either of them could protest. "Jenn, we kinda dragged you into this. You weren't a part of this from the beginning. Plus, I went home and took a nap while you were stuck over there. It only makes sense that you get the bed now. You were there the longest. You really need the rest."

She didn't even put up a fight. We were too tired to argue— also, just as I had planned.

"Alright," Jenn said. "As long as you think you'll be fine on the couch."

"Oh yeah," I said. "I could sleep anywhere right about now, too."

It was settled at that. We did a cursory job of picking up, vowing to get the rest of the mess in the morning. We also vowed to wake each other if we saw or heard anything off. Mr. Nightmare and John hadn't come for us yet, but it didn't mean they weren't going to come. We needed to get rest, but also to be ready at all times.

It didn't matter how tired we were, we said, we were a team and we were going to finish this off together. Going along with that was the hardest part for me. I didn't want to lie to their faces, but it couldn't be helped. Merrie went to bed first, Jenn followed a few minutes later, and I was left to lie on the couch.

One thing I didn't lie about was the fact that I could have slept anywhere. As I let my body sink into the couch cushions, I could feel sleep coming on fast, the exhaustion and the beers taking effect the moment my head hit the arm of the couch. My muscles relaxed and my body shut down. As I was about to let sleep overtake me, the thought crossed my mind to find an alarm. I didn't want to wake up the other girls, so instead, I got up and went into the kitchen. I got a glass from the cupboard and filled it with tap water. I drank it down, filled it, and drank the whole glass again. Then, I filled it once more and downed

JOE SCIPIONE

almost the full glass a third time. My stomach felt full, but I knew I'd still be able to fall asleep. I hoped having so much water in me—plus the beer—was enough to wake me up to use the bathroom in a few hours.

Full of water, I laid back down on the couch and fell asleep almost instantly.

I didn't dream at all and woke up needing to pee. The apartment was quiet. Through the sliding door I could see the sky beginning to brighten. The girls were going to keep sleeping until the sun was high in the sky. Not wanting to wake them up, I ignored the need I had to urinate and padded barefoot to the front door. I unlocked it silently and slipped out with my shoes in hand and the keys to the Dying Buffalo in my pocket.

Once outside I slid behind a bush, pulled down my borrowed sweatpants, squatted, and peed, hoping no one would be walking by. My legs burned when I tried to hold myself up steady, but I finished and made it back out to the path without anyone noticing. Then came the first part of the plan I was nervous about: The fucking Dying Buffalo. I couldn't travel on foot for what I had in mind, calling a cab wasn't an option because of the early hour, and there were no other vehicles to take. Which meant I'd have to take the Dying Buffalo. Don't get me wrong, I loved that car, but it was the worst thing to be driving if you wanted be stealthy. The car was the opposite of stealth.

Marcus's apartment was on the other end of the building and the windows looked out over the front, not the back where I'd parked, so I had that going for me. The girls were also extremely tired, which was good for me as well. I might be able to get the car started and leave without waking them. With any luck, the entire thing would be over before they woke up. I had to take my chances and go for it.

I opened the door and got into the driver's seat. I took a

deep breath, then turned the key. The Buffalo roared to life, making me question the entire plan. It was too late to change ideas now; I had come this far and needed to finish it. The Dying Buffalo and I drove across town to Prairie View, starting the second part of my risky plan. I needed to get into my Dad's shed without anyone noticing. The good thing was, if my parents did see me, I was fairly certain I could convince them to stay quiet about it until I was able to finish what I needed to do. It was one of perks of having parents who trusted you as much as mine trusted me.

I parked around the corner and left the car running so I wouldn't have to turn it on again in the still-sleeping neighborhood. Although it was still dark out, rays of morning sunshine were beginning to poke through the trees and it would be full light before long. I needed to get my tools and get the hell out of there fast.

As quickly and quietly as I could, I ran through Mr. Brunelli's back yard and cut between the row of shrubs separating his property from ours. Dad's shed was on the other side of the yard so I ran across, hoping neither Mom nor Dad were awake, grabbing an early morning coffee in the kitchen, because they would have easily seen me. When no one came running out of the house as I reached the shed, I popped open the latch and slipped inside. I grabbed a shovel and an axe, then left. I didn't even stop to re-latch the door because it would have taken too much time, and it sometimes made a loud metal clang Dad would have recognized immediately. From there, it was back through the shrubs, along the side of the Brunelli house, and back to the Dying Buffalo. The axe and shovel I carried into the front seat with me. I fed them through to the passenger seat and laid the handles against the headrest. With my tools acquired, I put the car in drive and drove off.

The first time I tried to take care of Mr. Nightmare on my own, I'd failed because I didn't know I couldn't hurt him. I'd been filled with rage then because he'd killed my brother and I wanted revenge more than anything else. When we were kids, I'd been talked into letting John kill Mr. Nightmare at the Dwelling, and that had backfired on me too. Now, I knew more about Mr. Nightmare—and the nightmare-eaters—than anyone else, and I had an idea I thought might keep myself, and more importantly my friends, from being hurt by them anymore.

It was time to return to the Shaw Farm once more and finish this for the last time.

CHAPTER 39

The sun was out when I got there. I pulled the car back into the same spot. This part of my plan was the only part that depended on someone else. I could do everything else myself, but I needed someone—hopefully Marcus, but if not, Mr. Nightmare or John would do—to bring me back once more to the Nightmare Realm. I couldn't do anything from this side. In fact, the job had already been done on this side by the tornado. The work I had to do needed to be done on the other side, and I couldn't get there without help.

I exited the car, then went around and grabbed the shovel and axe from the passenger side door. I waded through the debris that had once been the farmhouse. The time for looking out for stray nails and broken glass had passed. There was only about a fifty-fifty chance I'd return at all, but it was the best chance I had to keep my friends safe, so it was worth it. I maneuvered to what I felt was the right spot and stood still, axe in one hand, shovel in the other.

"Marcus," I said. It wasn't so loud I was shouting, but it wasn't a whisper either. If Marcus could hear me and could get there, I knew he would come. I waited and called him a second time. Then a third. I wasn't expecting success or failure, there were still two others I could call if I needed to, but I wanted to leave Mr. Nightmare and John out of it for as long as possible.

I sighed, ready to call John's name next, when the wind spoke to me.

"Not strong enough," the wind said. It was Marcus, and I'd been expecting it. He wasn't strong enough to come into our world, but I didn't need him to come to me.

"I don't need you here," I told the wind. "I need to go there, tell me where to go."

For a long moment there was nothing. I waited, hoping to hear the wind again, but there was no response at first. Then finally, the answer came.

"Fall forward," the wind said. I looked down at the pieces of house in front of me. Broken wood and glass lay scattered along with what appeared to be the front door. Nothing looked like a portal to another world. I had no choice but to trust Marcus. Holding the shovel and axe tight in my hands, I closed my eyes —oddly remembering a trust fall I did at college orientation— and fell forward. If I landed on the remnants of the house, I'd still live.

I didn't hit any of the wood below me. As I fell, the ground disappeared. I was surrounded by coldness, as if I'd jumped naked into a pile of snow. The cold was everywhere.

"I got you," Marcus said when the cold feeling dissipated. He caught me. In the dark depths of the cave. I opened my eyes and I was laying across his arms.

"Where's Merrie and Jenn?" he asked, as I worked to get onto my feet. I dropped the tools as I did so.

"Not here," I said.

"They know you're here?" he asked, but he knew the answer.

"No," I said. "I got them—and you—into this shit from the beginning. I'm not putting them in harm's way anymore. I'll fix this myself. With some help, of course."

"You're nuts," Marcus said. I couldn't look at his face, but something in his tone of voice told me he was smiling. "I have to tell you, Anna, I don't know how much time I have. They've been searching for me, and I keep getting these intrusive thoughts. Being like this changes you a lot faster than I realized. In good news, I have these instincts now. I know everything they know, I think. It's strange."

"I understand." I handed him the axe. "Let's make this quick then. If there's time you can tell me about those instincts."

"What's your idea?"

"This is the only place they—you—can come across. Right? At least near us, I mean."

"As far as I know, yeah," Marcus said.

"So, if we get rid of this passageway to our world," I explained, keeping one eye toward the empty cave—the last thing I wanted was visitors, "then they will have to use a different way in and out. It probably won't lead to us—or near us. John even said this is where Mr. Nightmare would come through, then he'd have to travel to us. They can't stay in our world for days at a time. They come and they feed and then they leave. If we get rid of this connection to our world…"

"They would have a much harder time getting Merrie, Jenn, or you," Marcus finished for me.

"Exactly," I said. "We tried to kill him and it didn't work. But this might be equally effective, if we can keep them away, I mean."

"Worth a shot," Marcus said. I handed him the axe.

He attacked the wooden wall of the cave with reckless abandon. John and Mr. Nightmare had ruined his life too. He wasn't going to live out the life he wanted with Merrie and I felt his anger with each swing. The wood was old and had the weight of who knew how much dirt on top of it. After a few swings some of the wood started to break.

"It's working," I said. Marcus gave a few more swings and two pieces of wood about waist high broke in half. Dust and sand sifted out through the space the broken board had once occupied.

"Dig that out," Marcus said. "I'll move over here."

He went a few feet down and started swinging the axe again, while I pushed the shovel into the dirt he'd exposed. After I moved a few shovelfuls, the packed dirt had loosened up enough that, instead of a little dust, it began to pour from the hole in the wall. As I got the dirt to begin to pour in from the first hole, a loud crack echoed down the cave. I looked over; Marcus had broken a second hole and was pulling at the wood with his hand.

"Go higher with the next one," I said, pointing to the top corner where the wall met the ceiling.

Marcus nodded and began again few feet closer to the entrance, while I dug at the second hole. There was dirt in the cave, but not as much as I'd hoped. I wanted things to go faster. I had no idea what happened after I'd left Marcus, but I didn't think Mr. Nightmare and John were going to let him do whatever he wanted to do. They'd come here looking for him eventually. We needed to be done when they arrived.

Marcus cracked another piece of wood, this one near the top, and the dirt came pouring out almost right away, hitting him in the face as he backed away.

"Can they—can *you*—manipulate the dirt?" I said. "Will they be able to move this dirt out of the way and recreate the hall?"

"No," Marcus said. His voice was raspy and he was breathing hard. "We can control the trees and some living things, but not the dirt or the ground. You should stay here, Anna. Stay with us. We'd be together again: you, me, and John. I'm sure Merrie would come and join us."

"Marcus?" I said. I glanced over at him, careful not to look at his face.

"Shit," he said. "Sorry. I told you these thoughts just come into my head. I don't know if they're being put there or if it's part of the transformation. I can overcome them, but it's getting harder. I didn't even realize what I was saying."

"Okay, let's keep going. You're going to have to get out at some point anyway. I'll stay in here and finish up." I forced the shovel into some more of the packed dirt and pulled it back toward me, releasing another flow into the shrinking cave.

"What do you mean?" Marcus said. He looked like he was ready to start chopping at another board, but stopped.

"You'll need to get out of here and I will finish it off." I knew what I was saying and hoped he would let it go. But of course, he didn't.

"You'd get crushed in here, Anna." He put the axe down and walked toward me.

"No, don't stop. There's no time," I said. "I know what I'm saying. I told you I was going to be the one who took care of this. Maybe I can't get back without you being with me. But I don't care. You, Merrie, and Jenn will be safe and I'll take care of this one myself."

"No," Marcus said. "You won't. Honestly, I'd rather die saving you three from all this shit than stay a nightmare-eater. And I can feel it getting closer every second. I won't be able to hold off these thoughts much longer. We'll cave it in together, then you can get back through me. The cave will be closed off and you—*all three of you*—will be safe."

"Marcus…" I started.

"No." He cut me off. "I not going to argue about this. You don't want me to live like John, do you?"

"No."

"Then let *me* do *this* for you. Just don't tell Merrie. Okay?"

"Fine," I said. It made sense. If it was me, I wouldn't want to live that way either. We'd spent too much time talking and needed to focus on our job if we wanted to get the cave collapsed.

Neither of us moved and the wood creaked inside the cave. It was working. The holes in the walls were weakening the entire structure. There might not be a whole lot of time left before the whole thing caved in. Marcus looked up at the ceiling. My eyes followed his. He took a massive swing and slammed the axe head into the wood. The board he hit split in half but didn't fall down.

"Hit it again," I said. "This place doesn't have much time left."

Marcus raised the axe and heaved its head toward the ceiling a second time. It made contact in almost the exact same spot. Dust rained down on us and the board split further, but still didn't crack all the way through. The more boards we broke and cracked, the sooner the cave would collapse. Even as Marcus prepared to drive the axe into the board again, the cave groaned under the stress of the weight above it. Marcus slammed the axe into the ceiling a third time and it was enough. Three pieces of wood dropped to the ground. Rocks, dirt and sand poured in around Marcus. He ducked his head and ran back toward me as earth flowed down in front of us.

"Ah, there you are." The loud, booming voice of Mr. Nightmare echoed down the cave. I could barely see because of the dirt and dust in the air, but I caught a glimpse of his top hat and John in his baseball hat, standing right next to him.

"I'm gonna get rid of this place," I shouted, and then started shoving the spade of the shovel up into the exposed dirt, causing it to fall faster. Then I turned to Marcus. "Keep going, we can do this."

"Stay with us, Anna," Marcus said, and this time he dropped the axe and reached for me. I swung the shovel at him and backed away. I didn't make contact on purpose, but hoped my reaction would make him realize what he was doing.

"Stay with me, Marcus," I said.

"Sorry, Anna."

"See, Anna-banana," John said. I hated him using my old nickname almost as much as I hated when Mr. Nightmare used it. "Even Marcus thinks you should stay." He and Mr. Nightmare laughed.

"You should stop destroying this cave though," Mr. Nightmare said. "We'll just rebuild it anyway. It will take no time at all."

There was concern in his voice. He was lying and it wasn't terribly hard to figure it out. He didn't want me destroying the cave and it made me want to take the thing down even more than before. Marcus must have heard the same uneasiness in Mr. Nightmare's voice because he slammed the axe into the ceiling above his head once again. The wood cracked and splintered. It felt like the entire cave shook. The dirt flowed faster; I covered my head. There was at least three or four inches of dirt on the floor that hadn't been there when I first arrived. The ceiling couldn't take much more of the assault. It would break soon.

Dead trees shot up from the ground directly below the hole Marcus had made in the ceiling. As they grew up, dead branches formed across the hole, stopping the influx of dirt into the cave. Marcus's hand flinched and the trees shrunk back into the ground. The dirt poured in once again.

I grabbed the axe and started to slam it into the walls. Mr. Nightmare and John got closer but Marcus held them off, throwing trees up in front of them like he'd done before. I had my back to Marcus, but this time I couldn't trust him to have my back while I kept working on weakening the cave. At any time, those insidious thoughts could take over his brain and he'd turn on me. He'd cage me or simply grab my face and force me to look at him. I'd be knocked unconscious and the whole thing would be over. I'd be stuck here, become a nightmare-eater for the rest of my life. But I continued swinging and Marcus kept John and Mr. Nightmare back. Sand rained down around us and filled the cave. The wood splintered and cracked even when I wasn't swinging. I looked down the long shaft; the roof was sagging right where Marcus had made the original hole in the ceiling, and I got an idea.

"Marcus," I shouted, while still slamming the head of the axe into the wall over and over. I could barely breathe and my mouth was full of dirt, but I didn't stop. "Grow the biggest tree you can right there underneath that hole and then get rid of the tree. It should be enough to collapse this fucking place."

I didn't look directly at him, but I could tell he was staring at me. Either he'd slipped back over to the other side and was getting ready to shove me down the cave toward Mr. Nightmare and John, or he wasn't understanding what I was saying.

"Marcus," I said. "Build the tree!"

There was no hesitation after the second time I shouted at him. As soon as I'd finished saying the words, a massive tree shot up from the ground right below the hole in the ceiling. When the trunk of the tree emerged from the ground it was as wide as the cave itself and it blocked any light that was able to make it through the haze of dirt particles in the air.

"Marcus," Mr. Nightmare shouted from the other side of the tree. "Leave the tree there, we can get in and the three of us can take Anna with us. We can get Merrie here too. Don't you want to be with her?"

"Come on, buddy." John's voice was friendly, not the voice of the being I'd heard since we first arrived in the Nightmare Realm. "We can be together, all of us. The Nightmare Club back together again. I know you want Merrie to be here. We'll get her to join us. They're scared. They don't know what it's like. It's not so bad. Is it?"

They did not want the cave to collapse. I coughed and wheezed as I sucked in more dirt with each breath. I couldn't see Marcus and had no way of knowing what he was thinking. I had to hope he was still with me.

"Marcus?" I gasped. "Take the tree away then get to me. I'll go back and this will all end. That's all we have to do and it will be over. They wouldn't be talking like that if this cave wasn't that important."

I heard my heart beating in my ears. My blood pounded through my veins hard and fast. The time we stood there while Marcus contemplated his next move was probably no more than a few seconds, but it felt a lot longer. I didn't know what he was going to do.

"Marcus," Mr. Nightmare shouted again.

"Marcus," a voice said from somewhere far away.

"Merrie," Marcus said. I knew she could hear him, like a voice in the wind. They must have woken up and, when I wasn't there, they knew where I'd gone. "I can't come there. But you can come here."

"No," I shouted. "They can't come here. We have to close this portal for good. Please get rid of the tree. The cave will collapse and this will all be over. Merrie will be safe."

He didn't hear me, and through my coughing and shouting I couldn't hear Merrie's side of the conversation. I also didn't know if Marcus was succumbing to those thoughts again or if he was focused on seeing Merrie. There was too much going on, and in the darkness, I didn't have enough information to figure things out.

"Just fall forward," Marcus said. It was the same thing he'd said to me.

"No," I shouted again, but I knew it was too late. Merrie was coming back.

CHAPTER 40

Through the darkness I heard coughing. Then Merrie's voice. "What's happening?" Merrie said. "I can't see anything. Where the fuck is Anna?"

"We can all be together, Merrie," Marcus said. "It will be great. The Nightmare Club back together once more."

"No," I repeated, but it didn't seem to matter. "Merrie, come to me. Marcus is having some issues right now."

"What do you mean?" she said. "What the hell is going on?"

As fast as I could, I explained everything I could to her, making sure to include how important to was to John and Mr. Nightmare that this cave remain intact. It wasn't the time to argue about why I left without telling them.

"So," I finished, "what I need right now is for Marcus to get rid of that tree. If the tree goes away, this whole place will collapse. Right before it does, we jump back through Marcus to get home and this portal to our world will be closed."

"Come on, Merrie," Marcus said. "Don't you want to stay here with us—with *me*?"

"You know I love you," Merrie said. "But I don't want to be with you in a place like this, Marcus. Anna doesn't want to, either. We want to be home and if you were thinking straight, you'd want the same thing for us. If you get rid of this tree we can go home and be safe again. Don't you want that? The person I love would want that."

Marcus shook his head. Whether it was to clear those sinister thoughts away or to remove the words Merrie was saying, I couldn't tell. There wasn't much time for me to figure it out because, as I waited for Marcus to make the right decision and help us escape, something burst through the ceiling above us. My first thought was that Marcus had created another tree there with the intention of getting the cave to collapse even faster. I was wrong. It wasn't Marcus creating this tree and it wasn't a single tree. Instead, six small trees had burst through the wooden ceiling at the same time. The trees were small and pressed tight against each other. They grew bigger, and while they grew, they formed themselves into a circle. Once in that circular position, the trees began to widen. I watched from below as the trunks got thicker. As they did, a small hole appeared in the middle of the trees. Above, I could see the red sky.

"You can't hide down there forever," Mr. Nightmare cackled from above us. Behind him I could hear the growling and snarling of the nightmare-wolves and I knew John wasn't far behind. They couldn't remove the tree Marcus had put in the middle of the cave without risking its collapse, so they needed another entrance and created their own. We had no choice but to cause a cave in now, or they would have the same access to the portal as they always had.

The trees grew slowly, pushing the dirt and ground out of the way. The hole between the trees grew also. It wouldn't be long before Mr. Nightmare or John would be able to jump down through it and join us.

"Marcus," I begged him, "we need you now."

"But Merrie is here, Anna," he said. There was no anger in

his voice and no compassion. "We can be together again. A group again. Join us."

The hole got bigger. Merrie pleaded with him. I groped around and found the axe. If Marcus wasn't going to help us, then when Mr. Nightmare or John jumped down, I was going to take the fight to them. I stood ready, hoping Marcus would remove all the trees and collapse the place, but it didn't happen. Instead, a nightmare-wolf jumped in through the ever-expanding hole between the trees. It landed on its feet and looked around at us. Eventually it focused on Marcus. John knew Marcus was our only hope and sent the wolf to take him out. If Marcus wasn't able to help us, Mr. Nightmare and John could take their time getting to us. I charged at the wolf as it sprang forward and latched its teeth into Marcus's side. He screamed in pain when the wolf clamped down. I recalled the discussion we'd had about the wolves not attacking us with as much violence as they could. When I saw the wolf land with its hind paws on the ground and begin to pull, tear, and twist at Marcus's flesh, I knew it wasn't just trying to hurt him, but trying to kill him. If the wolves had attacked Merrie, Jenn, and myself with the same intensity, we wouldn't have been able to make a return visit. Maybe now John was regretting not sending them to kill us from the beginning.

Marcus, though he was much larger and taller than the wolf, was pulled to the ground. There was too much movement for me to swing the axe wildly. I needed to be certain any blow I struck was going to find its mark. Marcus was trying to pull himself away from the wolf as it shook its head viciously from side to side. Then the wolf stopped tearing at him and held still, trying instead to tug Marcus straight back. Marcus dragged himself in the opposite direction. For a brief moment, there was no motion from the nightmare-wolf. I heaved the axe up above my head and was about the bring the sharp blade down on the front paw of the beast, when a second wolf jumped down, knocking me to the ground. The front paws of the thing hit my back and one of my shoulders. The axe slipped from my grip and landed on top of me.

"Anna!" Merrie screamed. I covered my head but the snapping jaws of the wolf clipped at my already injured arms and hands. I rolled onto my back and kicked my feet out, trying to get some distance between me and the wolf. The nightmare-wolf kept coming at me but I scooted back away from it while kicking my feet. My strategy worked until I kicked too close to the thing's mouth and the massive jaws closed around my foot. I screamed in pain. It felt like every bone in my foot was crushed by those powerful jaws. Once it had a hold of me, it didn't let go. I shook my leg and kicked out with the free one, but the beast tore and shook me back and forth like I was nothing. Behind my attacker, a third wolf jumped down and joined the fray.

"Anna, hold still." Merrie's voice rose up above the violence and chaos. It was difficult but I managed to keep my body still. I couldn't even see where she was, but I covered my head and prayed for the best. There was a dull thud and the tugging on my leg stopped.

"Got that fucker," Merrie said. I uncovered my head and saw the nightmare-wolf motionless, eyes staring off into nothingness as blood leaked from a wound at the base of its too-long neck. Merrie had already moved on. The other two nightmare-wolves were both pulling at Marcus. He was fighting them off as best he could but I could tell he was losing some of his vigor.

I tried to scramble to my feet but needles of pain shot from my foot all the way up my leg and ended at the small of my back. Merrie stood over the wolves, axe in hand, and slammed it down on one of them. The blow didn't hit true, but the wolf let out a yelp then walked away into a dark corner of the cave and fell down. Merrie raised the axe a third time and was about to hit the other wolf on top of Marcus, when another jumped down. I looked up at the hole and realized it was almost big enough for our tall, slender tormentors to join us. We needed

JOE SCIPIONE

Marcus to close the hole and collapse the place, but he was still fighting off the wolf.

I dragged myself over to the nearest wolf. I looked around for the shovel but couldn't see it. There wasn't time to search for it and I couldn't stand up to get a clean shot off with it anyway. Merrie brought the axe down on the wolf and this time she made solid contact. The wolf dropped where it was and stopped moving. At almost the same instant, I dove at the wolf tearing at Marcus's arm. I ended up on the thing's back.

I didn't know what to do, but acting on instinct, I wrapped my arm around the thing's neck. It was still biting and yanking on Marcus's arm when I started to squeeze. At first, it acted like I wasn't even there. I squeezed harder, pulling my fist toward me with my other hand and tightening my hold on its throat. The wolf's jaw relaxed and I kept my hold on it, bearing down as hard as I could, using my forehead to push the wolf's head forward while I cut off its oxygen. Marcus slid away and I screamed. The wolf dropped down onto its belly but I could still feel the tension it its muscles, so I held my chokehold on the thing.

"Marcus," Merrie said. "The hole."

I kept my hold cinched but watched as Marcus looked up at the hole. He groaned as he lifted his arm; the circle of trees above us disappeared. The large tree Marcus had put in place still remained. Dirt began pouring into the cave more steadily. Boards fell on either side of us and the creaking and cracking resumed.

"Come here," Marcus shouted. "I'll get rid of the other tree and send you back. They won't be able to use this place again. You'll be safe."

I dragged myself across the dirt as it piled up around me. Merrie grabbed my arm and pulled me toward Marcus. He was half sitting up, falling dirt hitting the face we couldn't look at directly. I got close to him and wrapped my arms around him, hugging him with my face against his chest. Merrie did the same thing on the other side.

"I'd send you back now, but I don't trust myself," he said between coughs.

"We have to do this together," Merrie said. Even in the darkness I could tell she was crying. She'd already left him once; now she had to do it again.

"Take care of her, huh?" Marcus said. He was probably talking to me, though I realized later it was quite possible he was talking to both of us—telling me to take care of Merrie and Merrie to watch out for me.

"I will," I said.

"I love you," Merrie said. He returned the sentiment and then looked at the tree. Dirt poured in around us and we were covered almost up to our waists as we sat on the floor. We'd be buried soon.

"Last meeting of the Nightmare Club," Marcus said.

That was it. There was no more talking. No more speeches or sentimental words of goodbye.

"Don't do it, Marcus," Mr. Nightmare shouted from somewhere beyond what I could see.

"Come on, buddy," John said.

They were too late. Marcus flicked his wrist and the tree shrunk back into the ground, disappearing and leaving a second gaping hole in the ceiling of the cave. More wood dropped from above. Behind it, what felt like the dirt of the entire world, dropped along with it. It didn't sift down to the ground this time, it fell in large heavy clumps.

"Hold tight to me," Marcus shouted above the sound of falling earth. There was no more cave. We were buried. I pushed myself into Marcus and felt Merrie do the same, like we were trying to climb into him. I closed my eyes and saw nothing but darkness. The earthy scent of dirt filled my nose. I couldn't breathe.

CHAPTER 41

And then I could breathe again. Fresh clean air filled my lungs. I coughed when I exhaled, spitting dirt from my mouth, then blowing it out my nose. It was dark. I had no idea what day it was, but I'd made it back to the destroyed Shaw farmhouse.

Merrie sat up next to me and looked up into the clear night sky. Behind us, a car door slammed shut. I lifted myself up and looked over one of the half-standing walls of the place. Jenn looked at us over the roof of the Dying Buffalo.

We should have been happy. The nightmare was over. Again. But there was too much lost. Last time it had been Chuck and John. This time it was Marcus. Last time, we'd made it out relatively unscathed. There were no major injuries to contend with once the fight was over. This time there were. Merrie's leg was chewed up and she had blood oozing from multiple small cuts on her head. My arm—which had once been wrapped neatly by Merrie—was unwrapped and bleeding again. My sock was soaked in blood; if my foot wasn't broken in multiple places, it would be a miracle.

Jenn came over to us. It was obvious she'd been waiting for

our return since Merrie got there.. She knelt down in the debris next to me and checked out my wounds, then did the same for Merrie. We didn't even try taking my shoe off to see how bad it was. At first, we thought we should go to the hospital to get it looked at, but none of us were ready to answer questions about what happened to us yet. Figuring the story out was going to take some time and some planning. Especially given the things people already knew about and the disappearance of Marcus. Instead, we figured it was best to go back to Marcus's apartment and let Merrie take a stab at diagnosing me. Merrie limped through the remnants of the house and made it to the car. I slung an arm over Jenn's shoulder and she helped me. I slid into the back seat, sitting sideways to keep my leg up across the bench. Merrie got in the passenger seat and Jenn drove.

"Do you think there's a chance Marcus made it?" Jenn asked.

Merrie shook her head. Thinking about the weight of the dirt on us, I agreed: there was no way Marcus made it out of there alive. I'd held my breath for a few seconds before being transported back to our world and sucking in fresh clean air. Marcus didn't have the same luxury. The amount of time it would have taken him to dig himself out of there *should* have made his survival impossible, but I'd seen my share of things that *should* have been impossible. I know why Merrie shook her head at the question. She shook her head because the idea of Marcus dying—giving his life to save us—made sense to her. She understood it because of the kind of person Marcus was. She needed it to be the way he ended his life. I wanted it to be true too. The best thing was for him to be there with us. If that couldn't happen, the next best thing was that he sacrificed himself for us. It was what we wanted to believe. But, even as Merrie shook her head no to Jenn's question, part of me wondered what else might have happened to Marcus. He—and John and Mr. Nightmare—had powers unlike anything I'd ever seen. They could do things no human could do. Was it possible Marcus was able to hold his breath longer? Was it possible that Mr. Nightmare and John were able to extricate him from the dirt? Yes, it was possible. I didn't know if it had happened, but I wouldn't have been surprised. I didn't say anything, of course. What good would it do?

We couldn't use Marcus's apartment as a home base for much longer. He was gone and never coming back. The longer we were around, the more people could see us and the questions would start. When we pulled into the parking spot, it was late enough that no lights were on in any of the surrounding apartments. Jenn helped me in and we pulled all the shades and shut the blinds. We only put on a few lights, we knew we needed to be quick. Merrie showered first, then I went. My foot was badly chewed up but Merrie was almost certain there were no broken bones. We got some food, ate, and then decided it was time to leave. Jenn had been missing for a long time. Merrie and I had been missing only a few days, but my disappearance took place immediately following another two-day stretch where I was missing.

In the end we decided to tell everyone we'd gone away, just the three of us, without telling anyone. It wasn't the best story, but it was hard for people to argue with. The only problem with it was we left Marcus out to dry and unfortunately, it was the only way we could keep people from asking us too many questions. The last people who'd seen Marcus were the people at his job. Merrie had been asking around for him, so it made it easier for our story to be true. We were heading away for a while and she wanted to let Marcus know before she left. When she couldn't get in touch with him, she decided to leave anyway.

If anyone wasn't sure about our story, they never said anything to me about it. That was the end of it.

* * *

We remained close and stayed in contact throughout the rest of the summer. By September, Pete and Mary's Bar and Grill had reopened and, even though I was teaching high school English full time a few towns away, I still managed to work Friday and Saturday nights with Jenn. Merrie was finishing up nursing school and was starting to look for nursing jobs at pediatrician offices in the area. The three of us still hung out at least once a week. We rented movies or ordered pizza, usually at Merrie's house because it was the biggest and had a finished basement. One night though, at the end of September, right when I started to notice the first changing of the leaves, Merrie called me with a different request.

"Hey," Merrie said, when I answered the phone. I had a stack of papers to correct and it was one of the few Friday nights I had off from bartending, so I hoped to get through the whole stack that night.

"What's up?" I said, still half reading the responses on the yellow-lined piece of paper.

"I already talked to Jenn," she said. "I wanna do something tonight. Will you come here around eleven thirty?"

I laughed. "At eleven-thirty I was planning to be in bed or asleep on the couch with a stack of papers on my lap, but for you, anything."

"Great," she said. "See you then."

The night passed and I actually made it through all of my papers and was sitting watching TV at around eleven-fifteen. Mom and Dad were asleep and I could feel myself starting to drift off. It was either get up and get moving or fall asleep on the couch, as was my original plan, so I got up. It was cool so I threw on a sweatshirt and a pair of old but heavy sweat pants, and left as quietly as possible. My foot had healed pretty quickly and I was back running on it within a few weeks. My arm was healed by then, as well. I walked around the corner to Merrie's house. She was already sitting on the front steps, the house quiet and dark behind her.

"Everyone asleep?" I asked, nodding to the house behind her.

"Yep," she said. "My mom still gets nervous I'm going to just up and disappear for a few days. I told her I came back fine and everything was okay, but you know how she gets."

"So, what's up?" I said.

"I'd rather wait for Jenn, actually," she said. "But I think you'll like it."

She handed me a flashlight. We talked for a bit about her school and how many classes she had left and what teaching tenth grade English was *really* like. When headlights swung around the corner, we both turned to watch Jenn pull in front of the house and park.

"Ladies," she said as she climbed out of the car, cigarette stuffed between her index and middle fingers. She came over to us, we hugged, and then she looked at Merrie and asked the same question I had asked.

"What's up?"

"It's been a hard time for me lately; though I keep trying to put on a happy face, I've been struggling," she said. The tone of the evening took and immediate shift. And—though I didn't think Jenn had put everything together yet—I knew Merrie's plan for the night. I'd known since she handed me the flashlight, but wanted to let her say what she had to say, so I kept the information to myself.

"So, I wanted to have one final meeting," Merrie went on.

"Meeting?" Jenn said.

"A Nightmare Club meeting," I answered, then looked at Merrie. "Right?"

"Yeah," she said, her voice soft and uncertain. "Would you guys come with me? The new, new Nightmare Club."

I didn't have to think about it. "Of course I'll go with you," I said, and put my arm around her waist, giving her a perfectly executed side-hug.

Jenn didn't say anything. There was worry all over her face.

I couldn't blame her. She'd been through too much shit the last few months because of us. If she didn't want to do it, I wouldn't blame her at all.

"It's okay to say no," Merrie said. "You've done enough. Even if you don't come with us, you're still a member of the…"

"I'll go," Jenn cut her off.

Merrie smiled, then climbed up the stairs to the front porch and grabbed two more flashlights.

"Follow me," Merrie said, shining the flashlight up at her face from underneath, the same way John had done on the very first trip out to the Dwelling. I smiled at that. I missed the old John and the way he used to take his hat off and push his hair off his face.

We walked the night streets with confidence. There had been a time when Merrie and I owned the streets at night. We'd felt like they were ours, and when we roamed the streets that night, we owned them again. While we walked, Merrie and I told stories of the Nightmare Club to Jenn. Not the sad stories, the fun ones. The stories which kept us close all those years later. We laughed while we walked, enjoying every second of reminiscing. We passed into the woods and trekked to the Dwelling. The old metal drum still sat in the middle of the felled logs. I understood now how Mr. Nightmare had created this place. He wanted to make it as easy as possible for us to be there. He wanted our stories, but most importantly, he wanted out nightmares. Merrie went over to the metal trash can and pulled something from her pocket. She messed around with it for a bit and then the contents of the drum caught on fire. Light from the flames danced on our faces. After a few minutes, I turned around and sat in my spot on one of the logs. Merrie did the same, finding her spot, and then Jenn joined us. She sat— without knowing—in a spot where no one had ever sat. We listened to the fire crackling and the crickets chirping in the otherwise quiet night.

Then Merrie broke the silence.

"Hey, Anna," she said. "Do you have a story for us?"

THE END

Made in the USA
Columbia, SC
20 August 2023

21903005R00140